THE SANTINA CROWN

Royalty has never been so scandalous!

STOP THE PRESS—*Crown prince in shock marriage*

The tabloid headlines...

When Prince Alessandro of Santina proposes to paparazzi favorite Allegra Jackson it promises to be *the* social event of the decade—outrageous headlines guaranteed!

The salacious gossip...

Harlequin Presents invites you to rub shoulders with royalty, sheikhs and glamorous socialites. Step into the decadent playground of the world's rich and famous.
One thing is for sure—royalty has never been so scandalous!

Beginning May 2012

Ben wasn't prepared for the savage blaze of jealousy that fired through him at the sight of Natalia standing so close to his client, their heads bent together, their lips mere inches apart. Perhaps they were planning to meet later for a drink—or more. The thoughts raced through his mind, exploded like fireworks.

Then Natalia looked up and he saw her eyes widen, her body freeze, and his doubts disappeared in an instant. He knew this woman too well. He *knew* her. And she wasn't flirting. Yet the realization that came on the heels of the first was far more alarming, far more frightening. Why the hell was he so jealous? Why did he care what Natalia did—or with whom? And how could he really know someone like Natalia, even if he wanted to?

"Ben…" she said, her voice little more than a whisper.

His heart was pounding, adrenaline racing through him from both the assumptions and unwelcome discoveries he'd made. They stared at each other, unmoving, transfixed, and the moment stretched into something taut and focused, as if they were balanced on a pinpoint, a knife's edge.

"I wasn't—" she began.

"I know," Ben said, closing the space between them in a few long strides. Then he did what he'd been aching to do for far too long. He kissed her. It wasn't gentle. It wasn't sweet or thoughtful; he didn't ask permission. He kissed her with all the raw pent-up fury he'd felt and had been feeling for far too long for wanting this woman at all.…

Kate Hewitt

SANTINA'S SCANDALOUS PRINCESS

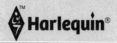

TORONTO NEW YORK LONDON
AMSTERDAM PARIS SYDNEY HAMBURG
STOCKHOLM ATHENS TOKYO MILAN MADRID
PRAGUE WARSAW BUDAPEST AUCKLAND

Recycling programs
for this product may
not exist in your area.

ISBN-13: 978-0-373-13078-8

SANTINA'S SCANDALOUS PRINCESS

Originally published in the U.K. as *The Scandalous Princess*

Copyright © 2012 by Harlequin Books S.A.

Special thanks and acknowledgment are given to Kate Hewitt for her contribution to The Santina Crown series.

www.Harlequin.com

Printed in U.S.A.

All about the author…
Kate Hewitt

KATE HEWITT discovered her first Harlequin® romance novel on a trip to England when she was thirteen, and she's continued to read them ever since. She wrote her first story at the age of five, simply because her older brother had written one and she thought she could do it, too. That story was one sentence long—fortunately, they've become a bit more detailed as she's grown older.

She studied drama in college, and shortly after graduation moved to New York City to pursue a career in theater. This was derailed by something far better—meeting the man of her dreams, who happened also to be her older brother's childhood friend. Ten days after their wedding they moved to England, where Kate worked a variety of different jobs—drama teacher, editorial assistant, youth worker, secretary and, finally, mother.

When her oldest daughter was one year old, Kate sold her first short story to a British magazine. Since then she has sold many stories and serials, but writing romance remains her first love—of course!

Besides writing, she enjoys reading, traveling and learning to knit— it's an ongoing process and she's made a lot of scarves. After living in England for six years, she now resides in Connecticut with her husband, her three young children and, possibly one day, a dog.

Kate loves to hear from readers. You can contact her through her website, www.kate-hewitt.com.

Other titles by Kate Hewitt available in eBook

Harlequin Presents®

To Meg Lewis and Anna Boatman, who helped me see this book through to the very end! Many thanks.

CHAPTER ONE

'Now there, at least, is a Jackson who has bettered himself.'

Princess Natalia Santina glanced at her mother, whose arctic tone belied what had sounded like a compliment. Queen Zoe's eyes were narrowed, her lips pressed together in disapproval. Her usual look then. Natalia turned to see who was the subject of her mother's grudging praise. Her gaze moved through the crowd of well-heeled guests who had come to the engagement party of her older brother Alessandro and his unexpected fiancée, Allegra, daughter of British tabloid fodder and ex-footballer Bobby Jackson, to finally rest on Ben Jackson, Allegra's older brother and self-made millionaire. Not that the money made a difference to her mother. Anyone, she liked to say with a sniff, could make money. Breeding was what mattered.

After all, the fiancé who had thankfully just broken Natalia's own engagement—Prince Michel of the small mountain principality of Montenavarre—hadn't had much money. He'd claimed Natalia had possessed impossibly expensive tastes, which was undoubtedly true for him. Prince Michel might be second in line to the throne but he was practically penniless, and in any case Natalia had no intention of spending her life in some draughty castle in the Alps, listening to her husband go on and on about his country's tediously noble history.

The question of just how she intended to spend her life

remained, as yet, unanswered. For the moment Natalia was simply glad to enjoy her reprieve from matrimony. Nothing in her experience so far had recommended it.

Now her own gaze narrowed as she took in Ben Jackson's powerful form. He was dressed in a well-cut grey silk business suit, his tie a sober navy, his movement restrained and precise as he chatted to another guest. Unlike his father, whose flashy tie, booming voice and expansive gestures proclaimed new money like nothing else could, Ben Jackson was the epitome of understated male elegance. Queen Zoe, Natalia had noticed with a stab of amusement, had held out only two fingers for Bobby Jackson to shake and flinched visibly when he'd lavishly kissed her hand instead.

'What does Ben Jackson do exactly?' she asked her mother, who stiffened at the vulgarity of such a question. Natalia knew you weren't supposed to ask what people did, because of course people of class didn't *do* anything. Not for money. Queen Zoe didn't even like to mention the successful business ventures of her own son and heir to the throne. Sometimes Natalia wondered if her mother had stepped from the pages of a Victorian novel, or even a time machine. Her attitudes certainly did not belong to this century.

'He's an entrepreneur, as far as I can tell,' Zoe said stiffly. 'Something in finance.'

How boring, Natalia thought, even as she eyed the oldest Jackson with undisguised feminine appreciation. The set of his shoulders underneath the tailored grey silk was impressive indeed. He lifted one long-fingered hand to make a point, his blazing eyes and set mouth creating an expression, Natalia decided, of controlled enthusiasm. He felt deeply, but he didn't want anyone to know. She'd always been good at reading expressions, and gauging a person's attitude. It had certainly helped her through twelve years of incomprehensible education, when often the curve of a mouth or lift of an eyebrow was the only clue as to whether she'd got it right or wrong.

'Who is he talking to?' she asked her mother. 'Ben Jackson, I mean?'

Her mother sighed with the kind of weary disappointment Natalia was long used to. 'He's talking to the minister of culture and tourism,' she told her, 'which you would know, if you professed any interest in or duty to the country of your birth and family.'

Natalia did not reply. She knew her mother was really referring to her recently broken engagement. Both her parents had wanted her off their hands and out of the country. At twenty-seven, happily unmarried and with a rather active social life, she was an embarrassment to the royal family. At least this time it was by choice.

'You're right, Mother,' Natalia said with as much docility as she could muster. 'I should be familiar with Santina's ministers. I suppose I'll have to remedy that immediately.'

And with a suggestive sway of her hips, she sauntered over to where Ben Jackson was still looking intriguingly… passionate.

The word slid slyly into her mind. Ben Jackson didn't look like a passionate man. The shoulders were impressive, yes, but everything about the man from his sober suit to his close-cut brown hair said restrained. Controlled. Boring, even. A man who guarded his passions—if he had them at all—carefully.

'Princess Natalia!' The minister of culture and tourism inclined his head in a nod as Natalia approached. She smiled, reaching out to shake his hand.

'Minister. How lovely to see you again.' The minister blinked, and Natalia wished she'd thought to ask the man's name before she'd come over. It would have added a nice touch.

'Likewise, Your Highness,' the minister responded after a pause, and still smiling, Natalia turned to Ben Jackson. Up close he wasn't quite so boring. His body radiated a certain leashed power, and despite his aura of restrained wealth and

prestige, Natalia still felt an undercurrent of cynical wari-
ness that intrigued her. He might have risen far on his own,
but he hadn't left the boy behind. But then, you could never
really leave behind the child you'd been…even if you wanted
to. Desperately.

His eyes were blue, navy like his tie, and now they were
narrowed not in admiration or even assessment but…amuse-
ment, Natalia realised with an icy pang of shock. He was
laughing at her. The thought caused a stab of irritation to
knife through her. If there was one thing she couldn't stand
it was to be laughed at. The butt of someone's silent joke. It
had happened too many times before.

'I don't believe we've been introduced,' she said, switch-
ing from Italian to English. She held out her hand, and Ben
Jackson's mouth flicked upwards at one corner, the faintest
of mocking smiles.

'Not formally,' he agreed, 'although I know you are one
of the Santina princesses, and you undoubtedly know I am a
Jackson.' He took her fingers in his own for the most cursory
of handshakes, but Natalia was still left with an impression
of latent strength.

'Ah, but which Jackson?' she replied with a lift of her
brows. 'There are so very many of you.'

Ben Jackson narrowed his gaze, his mouth pressed into
a thin line. Natalia gave him a bland smile back. She would
not be anyone's amusement. Not ever again. If she amused,
it would be by choice, not because of what she could—or
couldn't—do.

'And there are quite a few Santinas as well,' he replied in
as bland a tone as her smile. 'Large families are such bless-
ings, aren't they?'

'Oh, yes,' Natalia murmured, although she'd hardly call
her large family a blessing. Their relationships were too frac-
tured and distant for that. Save for her twin sister, Carlotta,
Natalia didn't feel particularly close to anyone in her family,

and certainly not her parents. Yet knowing what she did of Bobby Jackson's clan, she didn't think Ben thought his family such a blessing either.

The minister of tourism and culture had excused himself with a murmur, and Natalia nodded to his retreating back. 'You were certainly having a cozy chat with our minister. Are you planning on spending some time on our fair island?' She'd spoken playfully, giving him a flirtatious look from under her lashes, but Ben Jackson remained all too expressionless. Unaffected, or perhaps still amused.

'As a matter of fact, I am.'

'A holiday, perhaps?'

'Not quite.'

He was definitely amused. Natalia suppressed another stab of irritation. She was used to managing such conversations better, or, if she were honest, wrapping men like Ben Jackson around one manicured pinkie. No, not men like Ben Jackson. She had a feeling she hadn't met many men like Ben Jackson, which was something to be thankful for. The man was downright annoying.

'Then perhaps,' she suggested, 'you're here to keep an eye on your sister? Make sure she behaves herself?'

'My sister is an adult and perfectly capable of behaving herself,' Ben replied coolly, 'unlike some women who have been happily plastered across the pages of most of the tabloids of Europe.'

Natalia jerked back just a little, shocked by the sudden sharpness in his tone. He didn't sound amused any more; he sounded condemning. She knew she was featured heavily in most tabloids and gossip magazines. She sought out such publicity deliberately. Yet hearing this aggravating man mock her for the exaggerated stories of her evening exploits made her now burn with fury—and shame.

'Then you must be watching out for the rest of your family,' she said with an answering edge to her voice. She let her gaze sweep through the room, lingering pointedly on his outrageous father, who was laughing far too loudly, before moving on to one of his sisters arguing heatedly with a guest, and then another sister—some kind of reality TV star, for heaven's sake!—who certainly looked the part, before finally resting on yet another sister, a curvy blonde who was poured into a dress and flirting outrageously with a man twice her age. 'I don't believe all of them are able to behave themselves, are they?'

Ben's expression didn't change, not one bit, yet Natalia experienced a ripple of unease anyway. She felt again that impression of latent strength, leashed power.

'I believe,' Ben said softly, 'this is a case of the pot calling the kettle black.'

She lifted her chin. 'I hardly think we can compare families, Mr Jackson, despite their similar sizes.'

'Ah, I see. You're a snob as well as a brat.'

Natalia drew back, shocked. No one *ever* talked to her like that, at least not a commoner at a public event. Within the palace walls was another matter altogether. 'You should know,' she told him coldly, 'that I could have you thrown out of here for making remarks like that.'

'Is that a threat?'

Natalia said nothing. It *was* a threat, and a useless one at that. She could go and fetch one of the liveried guards standing sentry at the doors to the palace ballroom, and she could request that they eject Ben Jackson from the premises. Whether they would do so was highly questionable. Ben Jackson was the brother of the future queen of Santina and, despite his family's insalubrious background, an honoured guest. And the palace staff, on orders from her parents, took any of her requests with an irritating dose of cautious skepticism. She'd just been very foolish.

'Consider yourself warned,' she told him, and he laughed softly.

'At least you have *some* sense.'

'And you have no manners,' she shot back.

His eyebrows lifted once again, and another mocking smile quirked that rather mobile mouth. 'Kettle?' he reminded her softly. 'Pot?'

Natalia resisted the very strong urge to remind him she was of royal blood. And to kick him in the shins. Or maybe somewhere a bit higher. She plucked a flute of champagne from a circulating tray and took a large sip. 'So,' she said, eyeing him over the rim of her drink, 'why are you considering spending time on Santina?'

Ben regarded her for a moment, and then seeming to shrug although his shoulders barely moved, he decided—thankfully—to be civil. 'I'm starting a sports camp for the island's disadvantaged youth.'

Surprise flickered through her. She'd expected him to say something about touring Santina's sights, or renting a private yacht or palazzo. The usual reason a restless millionaire came to their shores. 'How very charitable of you,' she finally murmured.

'Thank you.'

'And I suppose you're hoping to find the next Lionel Messi or David Beckham? Get a few kickbacks?'

Ben narrowed his eyes. 'If you're implying that my aim in starting this camp is to find a future star and benefit financially from it then you would be very much mistaken.'

'Oh, come now. Surely you can't deny you have something of an ulterior motive? Or are you going to spend however many weeks or months setting up this little camp with no profit whatsoever?'

'As incredible as it seems to you, Your Highness,' Ben murmured, 'yes.'

Natalia shook her head. She knew enough about business—or at least men—to realise that no one did anything for free. There was always a price; it just depended on who paid it. And even if Ben had the saintliest motives possible, she still liked to annoy him. Especially since he'd annoyed her so much. 'Perhaps not a future star, then,' she acknowledged, 'but the publicity can't be bad.'

'You know what they say about publicity. No publicity is bad publicity, except I don't think that's quite true in your case?' He left it as a question, but the iron in his eyes made Natalia quite sure that he had no doubt about the publicity she'd had—or its accuracy. Only last week she'd been photographed leaving a club at 4:00 a.m., in the company of two well-known jet-setting playboys. A man like Ben Jackson probably found that shocking—and shameless. 'In any case,' he continued, 'the amount of publicity generated by a youth club on this small island will be negligible to my business or its profits.'

Natalia didn't know whether to be amused or outraged by his complete dismissal of *this small island*. She was a bit of both. Her mother would possibly swoon at such scorn. 'Well,' she said, keeping her voice careless, 'since you seem so well-acquainted with *the tabloids of Europe*, I have no doubt you'll be able to deliver the information into the right hands and guarantee yourself a front page or two.'

He stared at her for a moment, long enough to make her lose her edge of defiance and start to squirm. Or at least want to squirm. Thankfully she remained quite still. 'Are you always this pleasant?' he finally enquired.

'No, I'm not,' she told him. 'You happened to catch me at a good moment.' He let out a dry chuckle, surprising her. So boring Ben Jackson possessed a sense of humour. A small one.

'I shudder at the thought of catching you at a bad one,' he told her, and his voice was low and honeyed enough to slide right over her senses. Restrained and boring he may be, but he was also all too attractive.

Natalia knew she had been rather rude to him, but only

because she'd felt so defensive. As soon as she'd met Ben Jackson he'd examined and dismissed her, all in the space of a few minutes. She'd spent a long time perfecting her air of polished, jaded sophistication, and she didn't like someone like Ben blowing it. Seeing right through it. *Laughing* at her. 'Shudder away,' she told him. 'Somehow I don't think we'll be meeting again.'

Ben Jackson let his gaze sweep slowly over her—far too slowly, for Natalia felt not only as if he were seeing right through her, but stripping the clothes from her body. Not that she was wearing much. Her silver-spangled dress was haute couture but very short, with a plunging V neckline. She felt her body heat all over under his deliberate scrutiny, and knew Ben Jackson saw the revealing colour wash over her. Unfortunately she went blotchy when she blushed. Not at all the look she was going for, and a ridiculous response to a man who had treated her abominably. She needed to get out of here, before Ben Jackson saw—and knew—too much.

Ben watched Natalia flush with interest and a sudden kick of lust. She was a beautiful woman, he had to give her that. Sexy, sophisticated, with a wicked glint in her eye and a proud tilt to her chin. The dress she wore was outrageous. In other circumstances, he would have enjoyed suggesting they both get out of here and go somewhere a little more private. *Very* private. Yet he was quite certain, from what he'd read and now just experienced, that Princess Natalia didn't *do* private. Not like he did. He'd had enough scurrilous publicity for a lifetime, and he'd seen its effects tear through his family, a tornado of rumours and lies.

No, he had another suggestion for the princess. He watched her start to turn away, still proud, still bristling with affront, and he said, almost lazily, 'You can dismiss my football camp all you want, Princess, as some reprehensible publicity stunt, but I guarantee you wouldn't last a day—no, an *hour*—there serving as a volunteer.'

Natalia turned back, eyes narrowed to jade slits. 'I wouldn't *want* to volunteer even for an hour,' she snapped.

Ben grinned; he couldn't help himself. Sparring with her invigorated him, made him feel alive in a way he hadn't in a long time…even if she was completely annoying. 'That doesn't surprise me at all.'

'Let me clarify,' she said icily. 'I would not want to volunteer if you were present.'

'I bother you that much?' he enquired, and he couldn't keep the obvious innuendo from lacing his words. *She* bothered him. In more ways than one.

'I simply prefer not to spend my time with arrogant boors.'

He chuckled drily, reluctantly admiring that she never let up. Not for one second. 'You've summed me up quite quickly.'

'As you have me,' she pointed out, and to his surprise he thought he heard a thread of hurt underneath her magnificent disdain. The possibility made him feel uncomfortable, almost disappointed. He wanted to take Princess Natalia at face value, no more.

'Still,' he said. 'You should volunteer.' He didn't really mean it, of course. The thought of the princess swanning through his office, disrupting his efficient staff and generating all kinds of speculative publicity was definitely not something he wanted. Yet he couldn't keep from baiting her.

'Thank you for the suggestion,' she told him sweetly, 'but I'm afraid I'll have to decline.'

Now annoyance prickled under his skin, even though he knew he was being unreasonable. As unreasonable as the princess, refusing to even consider such a thing. 'It's so beneath you?' he enquired silkily.

Her chin lifted and her eyes glittered. 'You seem to think so.'

'I think it could be good for you.'

'Teach me a lesson? Thank you, but no. Go ahead and do

your little pet project, make yourself feel better, but leave me out of it.'

Annoyance turned to anger. Ben knew he was reacting emotionally to this woman's taunts, yet he couldn't keep himself from it, from feeling the anger surge through him at the way she'd dismissed not just him, but something that was so important to him. Already she was turning away. 'I'll make you a wager,' he told her in steely challenge, and she stilled.

'A wager? I don't gamble, Mr Jackson.'

'Please, call me Ben.' She smiled frostily and said nothing. He took a step closer to her. 'This isn't exactly a gamble, Your Highness. More a test of your mettle.' Her expression turned stony, and Ben knew what he wanted. He could handle the princess's theatrics, and even the publicity. Besides, with so much going on with the royal family, were the tabloids really going to jump on Princess Natalia for going to an office every day? And the thought of seeing her taken down a notch or two, or even learning something, was very attractive indeed.

As was she… For a second Ben questioned just why he was doing this. Then he thrust the thought aside, and dipped his head so he could inhale her surprising, citrusy scent, feel the feminine warmth of her only inches away. 'I'll bet,' Ben whispered, 'that I could convince your father to *make* you volunteer.'

She stiffened, half turned to face him, and if Ben had moved at all, their lips would have touched. He felt a jolt of lust, the depth and strength of his attraction surprising him, alarming him even. *Too much.* He could tell she wanted to take a step backwards, but she refused. She angled her head so she was looking up at him, and he could see the golden flecks in her eyes, a tiny mole at the corner of her mouth.

'Convince my father? I hardly think so.'

'Then you'll take the bet?'

Natalia eyed him coldly, and he knew she was torn between proving herself and staying safe. As was he… Just what was he thinking, inviting Natalia into his office, his *life*? Yet as her lashes swept downwards, hiding any emotion revealed in her eyes, he realised he didn't care. He wanted this.

'I didn't say that,' she finally said.

'Scared, Your Highness?'

Natalia drew herself up. 'You take the most appalling liberties, *Ben*. And no, I'm not scared. I'm just not interested. And I highly doubt my father would so much as grant you an audience, much less listen to your argument.'

Her resistance just made him want to push more. 'Then why not take the bet?'

'Why should I?'

'Of course. Something has to be in it for you.'

'Is there something in it for me?' she enquired sweetly. 'Such as you printing a public apology to me for your rude behavior in every tabloid newspaper from here to London?'

He laughed softly. 'What an odd thing to request. It's not as if anyone has overheard our conversation.'

'I'd still like to see you grovel.'

'I bet you would.'

Her eyes flashed and attraction sparked between them again, threatening to ignite to flame. Ben knew Natalia could feel it. He certainly could. Should he let her off the hook, keep them both from getting burned? He'd wanted to keep a low profile on Santina, and being involved in any way with Natalia would surely put paid to that. Besides the princess was exactly the kind of woman he couldn't stand. Yet still he said nothing, didn't move.

'You really are a betting man,' Natalia finally drawled. She shrugged as if she hadn't a care in the world. 'All right, go ahead and attempt to convince my father. You won't get very far. And if I win, and he refuses to grant your request...' She paused, and Ben waited, adrenalin coursing through him as if he were on the football pitch. This certainly was an even match. He couldn't wait to hear what she wanted from him. 'Then you are mine to command for a day.' *Command...?* Provocative images blazed through Ben's mind. Natalia smiled. 'Fair?'

'And if I win?' he murmured, his gaze heavy and intent on hers.

'Then I volunteer,' she answered with a shrug. 'And you get to command me anyway.'

She spoke without innuendo, yet it was there anyway. Desire pulsed in his blood, fired through him. He could handle it, Ben told himself. He could handle her. 'I look forward to it,' he murmured, and put out his hand for her to shake. He wanted to touch her. 'So we're agreed?'

Defiantly Natalia took his hand, and Ben saw her react to the touch of his fingers enfolding hers, saw it in the flaring of her eyes, that little hitch of breath. Then she smiled as if she hadn't a care in the world. 'It's a deal.'

CHAPTER TWO

'WHAT?' Natalia heard the outraged screech of her own voice echo against the walls of her father's audience chamber. He did too, obviously, for he winced slightly even as he lifted a paper from an ornate end table and scanned it with seemingly little interest.

'Please lower your voice, Natalia, and conduct yourself as a princess.'

Natalia nearly shook with disbelief—and anger. 'And princesses,' she asked, 'spend their days coaching football for the ragtag children of—'

'These children,' King Eduardo reminded her coldly, 'are the citizens of your country. You have a duty to them.'

'A duty to teach them football?' Natalia was quite sure her father and mother's duty did not extend much beyond the palazzo walls, unless it was making a speech or giving a little royal wave.

King Eduardo sighed and dropped the paper, turning to Natalia as if she were really rather wearying. It had already irritated her that he'd called her to him in this audience chamber, an ancient and ornate room that was meant for commoners to present their petitions to their king, not conversations within the family. Standing in front of him, the royal throne decked out in gold leaf between them, she felt at a distinct disadvantage. Still, she hadn't expected this.

'Natalia, the truth of the matter is, I think volunteering could be beneficial for you—'

'*Beneficial—*'

'Let me speak,' Eduardo said sharply, and Natalia, chastened, fell silent. She could not afford to anger her father now. 'You have been running around for far too long, living an inappropriate and extravagant lifestyle. I was willing to overlook it because of your impending marriage to Prince Michel, but since he has broken the engagement—causing some significant humiliation to our family—I see that other measures need to be taken.'

Natalia bit her lip, hard, to keep from speaking. She knew she'd been pushing the boundaries of her parents' acceptance with her partying. Of course, the tabloids exaggerated everything, but in her parents' world frequenting a nightclub was already skirting the perimeter of propriety. Yet what was she *supposed* to do? She didn't have a decent education, she couldn't work and she didn't fancy spending her days the way her mother did, dressing up for lunch, taking tea at a certain hour and waving at the masses from the balcony. And at least when she went out with a wilder crowd, she knew *that* was what the press would focus on. Nothing else.

'In any case,' her father continued, his tone utterly implacable, 'it has come to my attention that a bit of positive publicity could be very good for you, as well as this family. When I consider Sophia—'

'Sophia?' Natalia repeated, unable to hold her tongue any longer. 'What has Sophia done?' Sophia never did anything wrong. The press loved her, and her father had announced her engagement to Prince Rodriguez last night at Alex and Allegra's engagement party, to much acclaim. Unlike Natalia, Sophia was doing everything right. Wasn't she?

'Never mind,' Eduardo said sharply. 'The point is, I think your volunteering is an excellent idea, and I told Ben Jackson so. You are to start on Tuesday.' He turned to face his daughter, his dark eyes steely with determination. 'And do not think of defying me, Natalia, or you will find yourself without a penny, and an armed bodyguard making sure you do as you are told.'

Natalia swallowed. She was quite aware that her father's threat was real, unlike her own to Ben Jackson the other night. And the thought of being penniless and virtually imprisoned did not appeal to her at all. For a blinding second she hated being a princess, hated its restrictions and regulations, the oppressive expectation of royal duty, the secrets and shame she was forced to hide.

'Very well, Father,' she finally managed. 'I will do my best to be a credit to you and the Santina family.'

Her father waved his hand in obvious dismissal, and burning with frustration, Natalia swept out of the chamber. She stood in the opulent front hallway of the palazzo, half a dozen liveried guards flanking the various arched doorways. She could *not* volunteer for Ben Jackson. The thought filled her with a panicky fear that she couldn't bear to feel. Too much was out of her control. Too many possibilities of being humiliated, *exposed*—and by Ben Jackson, smirking in triumph.

The thought made her stomach churn and she felt physically sick. She had her reasons for acting the way she did, hiding in plain sight. She did not want Ben guessing them. Knowing them. Knowing *her*.

Natalia drew a deep breath and threw her shoulders back. Very well. If she could not convince her father to drop this ridiculous scheme, then she would have to convince the other man involved. She would talk to Ben Jackson himself.

Ben heard the gasps of shock from the reception area of his rented office and leaned back in his chair, smiling in anticipation. *That* had been quick.

A second later the door to his office burst open and Princess Natalia Santina stood there, her slanted hazel cat's eyes narrowed and glittering with fury. With her blond pixie hair cut and her long, lithe body, she looked, Ben thought, a bit like an elf. A rather naughty elf. He couldn't quite forget the image of her in that indecent dress last night. It had barely covered her bottom. Then she'd looked like sex in high heels; now she looked every inch the elegant princess, wearing a pink linen shift, high heeled slingback sandals and wraparound sunglasses which she'd pushed up onto her head. She also looked utterly furious. Ben smiled.

'Ah, so prompt, Princess. But I believe I arranged with your father for you to start on Tuesday?' He let his smile widen. He could practically see the steam coming from her ears. 'So consider this a twenty-four-hour reprieve.'

Natalia took a step into the room. Her chest heaved, although when she spoke her voice was level. 'You cannot really think,' she said coldly, 'to go through with this…this ridiculous idea.'

So she was going to try and play the princess card. Ben laced his hands behind his head and lounged back in his chair. 'Oh, but I can,' he assured her. 'Your father was really quite taken with it.'

'My father—' She bit off the words, looking like she wanted to chew them up and spit them out.

'Thought it would be good for you,' Ben filled in helpfully.

Natalia glared. 'I know what my father thinks, thank you very much.'

'Then there's no problem.'

She drew a deep breath. 'There is very much a problem, Mr—'

'Ben.'

'*Ben.*'

She was so very angry. Really, Ben thought idly, she looked rather magnificent when she was furious. Her eyes glittered and her cheeks were flushed, her breasts heaving underneath the snug pink linen of her dress. He could almost imagine what she would be like in bed.

Natalia Santina was a woman who gave as good as she got. The thought of matching her between the sheets had a distinct appeal…and one Ben knew he would have to resist. He chose his affairs with care and discretion, two words he could not apply to the princess. But he was looking forward to being her boss.

Natalia took another step into the room. She drew a breath and let it out slowly, smoothed her hands down the sides of her dress. Ben braced himself for a new tactic. 'Look,' she said, and her voice was pitched low, appealing. Sexy. He banished the thought and looked alert and interested, as if he might actually change his mind.

'I know we were winding each other up last night, but that's all it really was.' She smiled, playfully, and despite his best intentions to remain unmoved Ben felt his pulse kick up a notch. This woman really affected him, in more ways than he cared to admit. Again he questioned the wisdom of having her here, flitting around, smiling so sexily. No, he could handle it. He would stay in control. Always. He smiled blandly back.

'Was it?'

Irritation flashed in those hazel eyes. 'You know it was. I can't actually…participate in this camp of yours.'

Her tone invited him to share the absurdity of such a concept and, smiling regretfully, Ben shook his head. 'Oh, but you can.'

'But I'm—' She stopped suddenly but Ben could easily guess what she'd been about to say.

'A princess?' he filled in. 'And princesses can't get their hands dirty? Can't mingle with the masses? Can't do a single day's work in their bloody useless lives?'

Natalia recoiled, and underneath the anger Ben thought he saw a flash of vulnerability. Then she drew herself up, all haughty disdain, and he was reminded of just what a spoilt snob she really was. He knew what it meant to work. He knew what it was to try and fail and then try again. His father may have once been a famous footballer, but Ben had made his own money, his own life far from the scandal and notoriety of his upbringing. He'd earned the respect he now garnered; it hadn't been given to him simply because of who he was. Not like this princess. He'd be damned if he'd let her try to walk all over him.

'It's simply not reasonable,' she said, clearly now going for quiet dignity. A little too late for that.

'I don't see why.'

'Because—'

'Just what do you have against volunteering at my sports camp?' Ben asked, leaning forward. He genuinely wanted to know the answer. 'The children are generally friendly and well-behaved, and they can actually be quite a laugh. You might, heaven forbid, enjoy yourself.'

'You've done these camps before?'

'A few. One in London, another in Liverpool. Coming here was a way to launch possible camps all over Europe.'

'Ambitious, aren't you?'

Ben simply shrugged. 'So? What do you have against it?'

She stared at him and he saw something flicker in those hazel-green eyes, something that looked remarkably like fear. 'I don't know anything about football,' she finally said.

'It's not as if I'd expect you to coach.'

She didn't speak for a long moment. With the tiniest flicker of sympathy, Ben could just imagine how trapped she felt. Even he had been surprised at how readily King Eduardo had agreed to his plan. The rather dismissive way he'd discussed his daughter had caused Ben a ripple of unease. Natalia may be spoilt, snobbish, vain and even useless, but she was still the man's child. He had spoken about her, at least a little bit, as if she were nothing but a bother and embarrassment.

Finally she lifted her chin, settled her flintily determined gaze upon him. 'What would you have me do?'

Ben felt a surge of triumph, as well as a reluctant wave of admiration. The woman had courage. And pride. Too much of it, of course. He shrugged, spreading his hands. 'Whatever needs doing, really. Office work to begin with—'

'Office work?' For a second she looked panicked, which surprised him. Surely office work would be preferable to getting mucky with the children on a football pitch.

'The camp doesn't actually launch for another week,' Ben explained. 'When the Santina schools have their spring holiday. We'll start our first three-week camp then. Until it starts, you can help organise things here.' He gestured to the reception room out front that had been a hive of happy productivity, at least until Princess Natalia had stormed in and stunned them all into silence. 'You might not be able to type a hundred words a minute,' he allowed generously, 'but I assume you can handle a photocopier, do a bit of filing? *Read?*' He smiled, expecting her to laugh or smile back even if it was haughtily, but she didn't. She jerked her startled gaze upwards to his and for a second, no more, she looked terrified. Then her expression closed up completely and she jerked her head in what Ben supposed was a nod.

'We could make another bet,' he offered. 'If you can hack it here for thirty days—'

'*Thirty days—*'

'A month,' he clarified, and she narrowed her eyes to slits.

'I can count, Mr— *Ben*. Thank you very much.'

'Glad to hear it. Read *and* count. You're really quite accomplished.'

She said nothing, but her eyes blazed fury and something even deeper. Darker. Hatred, almost. The emotion in her eyes surprised him; the princess had been giving as good as she got. He felt a stirring of unease at the possibility that he'd actually hurt her.

'If you manage to stay the required month,' he said after a moment, keeping his voice mild, 'required by your father, I should add, then our original bet still stands. I'll be yours to command for the day.' Last night that had seemed an almost enticing possibility. Now Ben rather thought that if he was under Princess Natalia's command she would order him to carve out his own liver with an oyster fork.

She stared at him for a moment, her expression still closed and really rather remote, so he had no idea what she was thinking. It was almost as if she'd physically, or at least emotionally, retreated from him, so even though she still stood in this room, her lithe figure splendidly encased in the pink shift, she was in actuality a million miles away. Ben was surprised to feel a little pang of regret. Despite her aggravating personality, he'd enjoyed their sparring.

'You don't think I can do it,' she said at last.

He could not keep himself from replying, 'You have given me little cause to believe you can.'

Another flash across her features that he couldn't quite discern before her expression closed again. 'You don't know me.'

'I've read about you—'

'Do you really believe everything you see in the papers?' she scoffed, although he still detected a trembling thread of uncertainty underneath her disdain. 'Your family has been fodder for the tabloids plenty of times. Maybe you're the pot calling the kettle black now.'

Ben stiffened. He hated the kind of press coverage his family generated, had been trying to rise above it for, it seemed, his entire life. And he particularly hated any personal media exposure, having been dogged by it all too often when he was younger. Even now he could remember the look on his mother's face when she'd read the papers. She had never been able to resist reading them, seeing and even studying the photos of Bobby Jackson with his latest mistress. Seeing the photo of Ben himself, his tear-streaked face, only four years old. She'd let out a cry of anguish then that still reverberated through Ben thirty years later and made him avoid reporters and their invasive cameras as much as possible. 'It's true my family has fed the British press for far too long,' he told her evenly, 'but it's been my experience that even the most outrageous stories hold a grain of truth.'

'A *grain*.'

'Are you saying you've been maligned?'

She pressed her lips together. 'I'm saying I'll do it,' she finally said. 'Clearly I have no choice, and in any case I look forward to winning this ridiculous wager of yours.' She drew herself up, her eyes glittering, her cheeks high with colour. She really did look magnificent. 'I look forward,' she told him, 'to telling you just what you can do with yourself for an entire day.'

Ben let out a reluctantly admiring laugh. 'And I look forward to obliging you, I'm sure.' He reached into his desk drawer and pulled out the T-shirt he'd reserved for her. 'Here's your uniform.' He tossed it to her, and she caught it on reflex, staring down at it in incomprehension.

'It's a shirt,' he explained kindly. 'You wear it.'

She stared at the logo on front, her brow furrowed. Was she really going to object to wearing a shirt with his name on it? From what he'd already experienced of her, probably.

'Jackson Enterprises Youth Sports,' she read slowly. She glanced up at him, gave him a wicked smile. 'You've got your name all over this project, haven't you?'

'What should I have called it?' Ben snapped. He leaned forward, suddenly goaded into proving himself, even though he knew it was ridiculous. 'These camps mean a great deal to me, Princess, and I'd advise you not to stretch my patience too far. You have no idea what I'm capable of.'

She stared at him, the T-shirt clutched to her chest with one fist. 'And I'll say the same to you,' she said quietly. 'You have no idea what *I'm* capable of, Ben Jackson.'

* * *

Natalia stood outside Ben Jackson's office building, blinking in the bright sunlight and willing her heart to stop thudding.

Thirty days.

How could she do it? How could she survive? Ben Jackson's mocking voice echoed in her head, reverberated through her body.

Read and count. You're really quite accomplished.

He had no idea. Thirty days in an office would be a month of living hell. She'd had Carlotta's help to cover herself in school, but now…? How long would it take Ben to figure out her weaknesses? Mock them?

And yet despite the fear that coursed through her like liquid silver, Natalia felt something else just as strong: a blazing streak of determination. She wanted, more than anything, to prove Ben Jackson wrong. Annoying him in the process would be a pleasant bonus.

Her mouth curved into a grim smile as she imagined just how aggravating she could be to Ben. After all, he hadn't qualified his bet with any sort of progress or achievement on her part. All she had to do was show up and stick it out. And make his life miserable in the process…just as he would undoubtedly make hers.

And then, after thirty days, she would have won. Now she smiled with anticipation as she imagined what she would command him to do. Fetch her slippers? Write an abject public apology in the press? Have him follow her around like a lapdog? Another tantalising possibility slid through her mind, a sly whisper of just what Ben Jackson could do for her…and to her…

She pictured those broad shoulders and trim hips, those eyes darkened with desire…those long-fingered hands roving over her body with languorous intent. Then she pushed the images away. No, she had no interest in that. Ben Jackson was too autocratic and arrogant to be anything but her boss. Besides, she might flirt and date and have it written up in a tabloid as a torrid affair, but in reality she was very choosy with her relationships. That was one lesson she'd learned all too easily.

The smile died from her lips as she considered what lay between her and winning the wager. Thirty days. Thirty days of working hard—Ben would do his best, she knew, to keep her nose to the grindstone. She sighed, her shoulders slumping before she drew herself up again. She wasn't afraid of working hard. She just didn't know if it could produce any meaningful result.

Back at the palazzo Natalia was surprised to find her father closeted with a handful of advisers and her mother in a ferment of anxiety. She asked for Natalia to come to her private rooms upon her return, which she did. Despite her party-going antics, Natalia had yet to disobey a direct order.

'What's going on?' she asked, and Queen Zoe raised perfectly plucked eyebrows.

'What's going on? Only that your foolish sister has run off!'

Natalia slid her sunglasses up onto her head. 'Sophia?' she guessed, thinking of her father's words this morning. Her own twin, Carlotta, had already shamed the Santina family by having a child out of wedlock and was trying to live a quiet life in Italy. Natalia didn't think on top of that she'd just disappear.

'Yes, Sophia,' Zoe said with a worried huff. 'Apparently she would rather ruin her reputation than marry Prince Rodriguez.'

'Really,' Natalia said, and didn't even bother sounding surprised. Wasn't she the same? She just hadn't possessed the courage to take it as far as Sophia apparently had done. 'Where has she gone?'

'She has stowed away on the airplane of the Maharajah Ashok Achari.'

'Ash?' Natalia said incredulously. Ash was one of her brother Alex's oldest friends, and as such had visited the

palazzo several times. Sophia, Natalia suspected, had always had a bit of a crush on him. But to stow away on a plane…! She felt a thrill of admiration as well as envy. She might have made a few scenes, caused a few minor scandals, but she'd never done something really brave.

'The media is going wild,' Zoe said in disgust. Both of her parents hated the press, though they recognised the need to appease the people's desire for press coverage of the royal family. 'Between this and how they've taken to Alex's intended—' Her mother stopped abruptly. 'Really, I cannot conceive what your sister was thinking.'

She'd taken her future into her own hands—in a way Natalia never had.

Zoe sighed. 'The media is having a field day with Alex's choice of bride and now Sophia and Ash are having a hasty, patched-up wedding. Your father was quite right in having you volunteer for the Jackson boy. In these precarious times we must do what needs to be done.'

Ah, Natalia thought, royal duty. Of course.

Zoe turned to Natalia, her expression now one of kindly appeal. 'I know this volunteering might be a bit…difficult for you,' she said, and Natalia stiffened. Her mother's sympathy was far worse than her scold. 'But the positive publicity really is important now.' She smiled sadly and spread her hands wide. 'We're depending on you, Natalia.'

CHAPTER THREE

NATALIA stood in front of Ben Jackson's office building on one of the best streets of the business district and took a deep breath. She'd had a fraught morning. The palazzo was still in uproar over Sophia and Ash's scandalous elopement, and the paparazzi had hounded Natalia all the way to the door of the chauffeured car that would take her into the city. Fortunately the driver, Enrico, had lost them on the winding, cobbled streets of Santina's capital city and now Natalia was left mercifully alone. But not for long. News of her volunteering would leak out and then she would be hounded again. She could just imagine how the press would handle her sudden charitable streak. *Bad Girl Plays at Being Good.* No one would take it at face value, or consider it admirable. She knew that. Her mother might be depending on her to bring in some good press, but Natalia doubted she could be the one to do it.

Sophia had always been the darling of the media, and even Carlotta's sins were quietly forgiven, since she was so obviously repentant. But Natalia? She was the party girl—shallow, selfish, reckless and wild—and the paparazzi had no desire for her to shake off her role. Neither, it seemed, did Ben Jackson. From their conversation two days ago, Natalia suspected he was quite looking forward to seeing her fail. She straightened her shoulders and started towards the office. Today she would begin proving him wrong...and making his life hell in the process.

'You're late.' Natalia had just stepped into the building when Ben appeared in his own office doorway, tapping his gold and silver watch. 'Ten minutes after nine, Princess.'

'Please, call me Natalia,' she said with exaggerated graciousness. 'Or if you prefer, Your Highness.'

Ben's lips twitched even as he narrowed his eyes. 'We're informal in this office. Everyone will call you Natalia.'

Natalia glanced at the three people working in the front office, two women and a man, all of their mouths agape, their eyes as wide as saucers.

'And,' Ben continued, his voice hardening, 'everyone arrives on time.'

'Of course,' Natalia replied smoothly. 'It's just that I had some difficulties avoiding the press. They were parked outside the palazzo all morning. And not on my account, I might add.' She gave him a smilingly pointed look as she took off her light silk trench coat and held it out. The woman behind the receptionist desk hurried to take it and Ben's face darkened.

'You can hang up your own coat,' he snapped, and Natalia inclined her head in regal acknowledgement. She had a feeling that playing the gracious royal would get right up Ben's nose. And in actuality, she'd held out her coat unthinkingly. She was used to someone snapping to attention any time she needed or wanted something; that was how things had always been done in the palazzo. Clearly it was not going to be like that here.

She registered the narrowing of his eyes and the flare of awareness as he took in her clothes; she'd worn the T-shirt he'd given her but paired it with a pale grey silk pencil skirt and matching cardigan, and finished the outfit with a narrow belt in black patent leather and a pair of very high heels. Everyone else in the office wore jeans, save Ben, who was dressed in another sober suit. The man, Natalia thought idly, wanted to appear strait-laced. Boring, even. But she didn't think he was, underneath. Not if that flaring in his eyes was anything to go by. A lot of emotion bubbled underneath that coolly arrogant facade.

Ben introduced her to his staff: Francesca, a competent-looking young woman in her twenties; Mariana, a stout matron in her early forties, and Fabio, a shy young man who blushed crimson as he stammered his hello. They were all islanders, all bilingual, and they all, of course, knew exactly who she was. Natalia greeted them graciously, but she saw the mix of awe and speculation in their faces and wondered what they thought of her. What they'd read, and what they believed. Not that she cared. She wouldn't let herself.

'Come into my office,' Ben said, still sounding annoyed, 'and you can get started.'

'*So* lovely to meet you,' Natalia told the three still standing with their mouths agape, and they stammered their replies. She strolled into Ben's office and he closed the door firmly behind her.

'You can drop the princess act,' he growled, and she turned around, arching her eyebrows.

'But I am a princess.'

'You know what I mean. As long as you're here, *Your Highness*, you're just another one of my employees.'

'Volunteers,' Natalia corrected sweetly, and Ben's eyes narrowed to near slits.

'Very well. Volunteer. And my employees out there are not your royal subjects as long as we're in this office.'

'So you object to my being polite?'

'I object to you acting like you're *gracing* us with your presence,' he snapped.

'Oh, I see,' Natalia said, sitting in the chair across from his desk and crossing her legs neatly. 'You want me to grovel.'

Ben let out an exasperated breath. 'I just want you to act… normal.'

'This is normal for me.'

'Really?' He looked irritatingly skeptical. 'Somehow,

Princess, I don't think any of this is within the realm of your normal activities.' He glanced pointedly at her demure outfit, and Natalia knew he was thinking of the rather outrageous outfit she'd worn at the engagement party. It had been a *very* short dress.

Natalia gave him a cool look. She would not let him rile her, even though her heart had already started thudding hard both with anger and trepidation. She *was* outside of her realm of normal activities. And her comfort zone. 'Tell me, Ben,' she asked in as friendly a tone as she could manage, 'why do you want me here? To teach me a lesson or to have me actually help?' His eyebrows snapped together, but he said nothing. 'Because,' Natalia continued, leaning forward, 'if I'd offered to help without you first arranging this ridiculous bet, I doubt you'd be scolding me in front of your staff and calling me "princess" in that sneering voice.' She saw realisation and something close, perhaps, to regret cross his features, darkening his eyes and tightening his mouth.

'But you didn't,' he finally said, biting off the words.

'So I'm to be punished?'

'I'm just treating you like everyone else who works here, Prin— Natalia.'

'Ah, with respect and courtesy then.'

For a second he looked completely flummoxed, and Natalia felt a savage surge of satisfaction. He may have got the better of her in their last conversation, but she was determined to give as good as she got today. She smiled, her point made, and leaned back in her chair. 'How long has this office been going?'

He looked surprised by the turn in conversation, but he took it in his stride. 'About six weeks.'

'And you've been here that whole time?' How had she not come across him before?

'No, I flew in for a couple of days, that's all. But now I'm going to be on site for the running of the first camp, before I return to London.'

'What a coincidence,' Natalia murmured, 'that your sister is now engaged to the country's future king.'

'Not that much of a coincidence. I knew Alex was in London. I met with him about this camp, so it's not too much of a leap of the imagination to think he came across Allegra.'

'And proposed on the spot?'

'I met with him months ago,' Ben explained coolly. 'They obviously had a few months of dating. And,' he finished with a dismissive shrug, 'when you know, you know.'

Obviously he didn't like anyone casting doubt on any of his family. The man was amazingly sensitive about his unruly clan. 'You know?' she repeated. 'Are you talking about true love?' She imbued the words with as much skepticism as she felt.

Ben's face remained expressionless. 'Obviously you don't believe in it.'

'Do you?'

'We hardly need to discuss my feelings on the matter,' Ben said crisply. 'You're here to work, not gossip.'

She uncrossed her legs and straightened in her chair. 'Very well.' The fact that he hadn't answered intrigued her, even though she knew it shouldn't. What on earth did it matter what Ben Jackson thought about true love? She certainly didn't believe in it, not after seeing the enduring frosty civility between her parents, and Carlotta's heart being trampled on by that no-good ambassador. Not to mention her own foolish attempt at a real romance. She had no time or interest in love, true or otherwise...which was why she'd been so relieved to have her own engagement broken.

Ben rose from his chair, and so did Natalia. 'Francesca will be in charge of your duties in the office,' he told her. 'Next week, when the camp starts, you'll report directly to me.' Did he say those words with rather grim relish, or was Natalia just imagining it?

She gave him her most saccharine smile. 'As you wish.'

'Music to my ears,' Ben murmured, and led her back out to the front office.

The first few hours of Natalia's enforced volunteering went, to her relief, surprisingly smoothly. Francesca gave her a large pile of photocopying to do, and operating the machine was well within Natalia's abilities, albeit rather tedious. Still the monotony was made bearable by the presence of the others, who kept up a stream of cheerful chatter about books and films and summer plans, to which Natalia contributed, although her intent to cruise the Cyclades on a friend's private yacht left them all silent, as did her airy admission that she'd seen the film they were discussing at its world premiere in Cannes last year. Natalia didn't talk so much after that. Ben kept himself closeted in his office, so at least she didn't have to endure his scowling observation.

By the time lunch rolled around Natalia was starving and exhausted. It annoyed her that one morning tired her out, but she decided that everyone could use a break, and she offered to take her three colleagues out to lunch.

'We usually just have sandwiches—' Mariana said, and Natalia waved this aside. After being cooped up in an office the whole morning, they all deserved a treat.

'But you do get a lunch hour, don't you?'

'Yes—'

'Then it's settled,' Natalia said firmly. 'Why don't we just leave Mr Jackson a note?' Ben, thankfully, had gone out earlier to a meeting and Natalia was grateful not to encounter him now. He'd only have something sardonic to say.

Francesca wrote the note and Natalia took them all to one of her favourite restaurants, a little Italian bistro on a back street that looked unassuming but had a six month waiting list for reservations. Fortunately they always had a table reserved for a princess.

'Order whatever you like,' she told everyone, and asked for a bottle of very nice wine to be brought to the table. She was just raising her glass in a toast to her colleagues when a hush fell over the table and she saw a shadowy figure darken the doorway of the bistro. *Ben.* And he looked furious.

'Join us,' she offered airily as he approached the table. 'I was just about to propose a toast.'

'What a surprise,' Ben drawled. 'Please. Continue.' And smiling, although his eyes still glittered ice, he accepted a glass.

'To a fabulous first day of work,' she said, a bit defiantly, and after clinking glasses with everyone she drained her own. She could feel Ben's gaze on her, narrowed and speculative, over the rim of his own glass. He dropped into the seat next to her.

'Don't you mean a fabulous first morning of volunteering?' he said dryly, leaning forward so his lips almost brushed her ear. His breath fanned her skin and she felt an entirely unreasonable and yet undeniable reaction to him, a shivery heat stealing through her body.

She turned to give him a breezy smile, but he was too close. Far too close. She stilled, and her gaze dropped to his lips, so mobile and sensual, so unlike the rest of his face, all harshly defined planes and angles. 'Whatever you like to call it,' she replied, meaning to sound flippant but her voice was too husky. His gaze still locked with hers, Ben took another sip of his drink.

'Cheers, then,' he said.

Natalia had ordered half a dozen of her favourite dishes, yet with Ben lounging next to her she found she could barely manage a mouthful. There was something so…distracting about his presence, his overwhelming maleness. Even in his sober suit he exuded a masculine assurance and even arrogance that made Natalia fumble with her fork, the delicious food dry in her mouth. What was it about this man? And how had she ever thought he was boring?

When the waiter brought the pistachio cannoli for dessert Ben looked pointedly at his watch. 'As delicious as this all looks, your Highness, I'm afraid we've been at lunch for well over an hour and there is work to do.' He smiled at the waiter, although his eyes flashed dark fire. 'Do you think we could get that wrapped up?'

Natalia bit her lip, suddenly feeling ridiculous. Clearly this lunch had been a little over the top. The rest of Ben's employees must have thought so too, for they were a rather sorry, silent little crew as they trooped back to the office.

Natalia was just dragging her feet towards the photocopier when Ben paused in the doorway to his private office, eyebrows lifted. 'Natalia? Could I see you a moment in my office?'

Her stomach flipped and her heart did a somersault. Was he about to bawl her out, again? 'Of course.'

Head held high, she sailed past Ben into his inner sanctum, heard the click of the door closing behind her.

'That was quite a show,' he said, mildly enough, but Natalia still heard the steel underneath.

'It was lunch.'

'Perhaps in your world, Princess—'

'Natalia—' she corrected firmly.

'But the average office worker doesn't have a two-hour lunch complete with lobster and champagne.'

'Wine, actually.'

He narrowed his eyes. 'If you're going to work here—'

'But I don't work here,' Natalia pointed out. 'I volunteer.'

'You are under my authority,' Ben bit out, 'and I will not allow you to swan into my office and do your la-di-da routine instead of properly working!'

Smiling, Natalia planted both her hands on Ben's desk and

leaned forward so their faces were mere inches apart. 'Then maybe,' she suggested softly, 'you should have thought of that before you made that bet.'

Ben stared at her for a long moment and Natalia became tantalisingly conscious of how close they actually were. If she just leaned forward a little bit, she could kiss him. She imagined the feel of his lips on hers. Would they be hard or soft, yielding or resisting? Would he take control of the kiss, deepen it into something more? She felt a plunging sensation in her stomach, as if she'd missed a stair. She thought he would be a masterful kisser, and she realised she very much wanted to find out.

Her breath hitched and her heart began to thud with hard, heavy beats. It would be so easy…and yet so impossible. She was already playing with fire, taunting him like this. She didn't want to get completely singed. She knew how that felt, and it wasn't pleasant.

Ben finally leaned back in his chair, nodding slowly, his eyes narrowed with steely understanding. 'I see what this is. Your little revenge.'

Natalia shrugged, saying nothing. Her heart was still thudding hard and in truth she couldn't say what *this* was. She'd arrived this morning fully intending to annoy Ben by playing the spoilt brat, yet how could you play at something you actually were? She kept getting muddled, not sure what was pretend and what was just her. And as for the lunch… Another twinge of embarrassment assailed her. She'd actually meant it as a kindness. She'd *liked* chatting with Francesca, Mariana and Fabio, and providing lunch had seemed like something she could do, something they would enjoy. Yet when Ben had joined them, looking so disapproving and disdainful, she'd overreacted on purpose just to annoy him. Clearly she'd succeeded.

Staring at him now, his expression so assessing and judgmental, Natalia felt an uncomfortable welter of emotions—

regret and defiance, hurt and pride. Everything was confused. *He* was confusing. And now he was glaring at her quite ferociously.

She straightened, taking her hands off the desk and smoothing her skirt. 'Shall I get back to work now?' she asked, scrupulously polite, and Ben let out a humourless laugh.

'You mean volunteering, don't you?' he said, and waved towards the door. 'By all means. Waste everyone's time for another few hours.'

Back in the front room Francesca, her eyes cast down and her expression meekly contrite, handed Natalia a large stack of files. 'These can go in that drawer over there,' she said, indicating an ugly, iron-grey filing cabinet in the corner.

'You have this many files already?' Natalia asked, trying to suppress a little flutter of fear. 'I thought this office had only been around a few weeks.'

'Nearly a month,' Francesca replied, 'but there is a lot of paperwork. Legal matters, insurance—'

'Right.' Natalia turned towards the cabinet. 'So where do these go?'

'You put them in alphabetically,' Francesca explained. 'See how they're labeled?' She pointed to a neatly printed label on each file and then opened the top drawer of the cabinet. 'It's pretty self-explanatory. Just look for the corresponding file in the cabinet.'

'Right.' And it was simple, Natalia knew. That didn't mean it was easy. Francesca walked back to her desk and Natalia put the stack of files on top of the cabinet. She swallowed, straightened her skirt. She would just take this one file at a time and work slowly. Carefully. Yet staring at the tottering stack of files on top of the cabinet, she felt working through them was akin to scaling Mount Everest. In bare feet.

The mood of the office was subdued for the next hour, which didn't help Natalia's painfully slow process through the files. Ben strode out of his office, gave Natalia and her files a sharply assessing look before announcing that he was going out for a bit.

The mood lightened a bit after that, and they all started chatting again, which made things easier. In fact, Natalia was just describing the gown she'd worn to a royal ball, her audience quite captivated, when Ben came back to the office.

'Three rows of seeded pearls sewn along the hem, which actually made it ridiculously heavy. I think I lost five pounds wearing that thing.'

Ben didn't speak, but she felt his tension. His annoyance, or maybe even his anger. 'Natalia,' he said, scrupulously polite, 'could I please see you in my office?'

Again? 'Of course,' she said as airily as she could, and turned away from the filing cabinet. 'Twice in one day I've been called to the headmaster's office,' she quipped once he'd closed the door. 'Must be my lucky day.'

'Or mine,' Ben replied dryly. He leaned against the door, his arms folded, his expression turning heavy-lidded. He had amazingly long lashes, Natalia noticed rather absently. On another man those lashes, sensual lips might seem effeminate, but Ben was far too potently male for that. His whole body radiated strength...and tension.

'Are you amusing yourself, Princess, working as slowly as you can? Sending my entire office into a tailspin?'

'Infuriating you is my main purpose, actually,' Natalia replied, 'although it is amusing, which is a bonus.'

Ben's eyes narrowed even though he still leaned lazily against the door. 'And is that how you plan on spending the entire month?'

'We-*ell*,' Natalia drawled, 'it will probably become boring before then. I'll have to change tactics at some point.'

Ben stared at her hard for a moment, and Natalia lifted her chin. She would never admit how hard her heart was beating, how weak and vulnerable and *scared* she felt, having had to work through that pile of near-incomprehensible filing, and then to have Ben see how pitiful she was. She'd rather die than have him know any of it. Any of her weaknesses.

After a tense, silent moment he let out a reluctant laugh. 'You really are amazing.'

'Thank you.'

'I'm not sure I meant it as a compliment.'

'I'll take it as one, anyway.'

He laughed again, shaking his head. 'Seriously, Natalia.' Something skittered across her spine and then dove right into her heart at the sound of her name on his lips. Not a mocking *princess*, or a sardonic *Your Highness*. Just her name. Who she was.

'Seriously?' she repeated. 'You want to be serious?'

'I know it goes against your nature.'

'Of course it does.'

'It's going to be a long month if you keep this up.'

She smiled and shrugged, but somehow she couldn't quite manage a comeback quip. Not now. Not about this. Because the truth—the truth she never, ever wanted Ben Jackson to know—was she'd been trying as hard as she could with that stupid filing.

'I know you want to get back at me,' Ben continued, 'and God knows, maybe I deserve it.'

'It isn't just God who knows.'

His mouth kicked up at the corner, and Natalia felt her heart beat even harder at the sight of his smile. 'Still, for the sake of the children—'

She arched an eyebrow. 'The children care about filing?'

'You know what I mean.' He spoke quietly, his voice thrumming with sincerity, and Natalia felt a twist of emotion inside, a softening and longing she couldn't bear to feel. She shrugged again.

'Like I said, I'll have to change tactics. I get bored easily.'

He frowned, cocking his head, and Natalia had the strange

sensation that he didn't believe her. That he suspected she was lying, hiding—and she couldn't have that.

Quickly she turned towards the door. 'Is that all, Captain?'

'For now.'

With a mock salute she disappeared back into the front room, and faced the files this time with a sigh of almost-relief. Ben Jackson was far too perceptive for her own comfort...or safety.

Ben stared at the door Natalia had just disappeared through, closing it firmly behind her, and frowned. That woman got under his skin. More than he liked. She annoyed and intrigued and invigorated him all at once, and it made him uneasy. Even a little angry. Women didn't get close to him; no one did. Getting close meant losing control, and that was something Ben never did.

Yet from the moment Natalia had breezed into his life, she'd been chipping at the self-control he prided himself on. The cornerstone of who he was, for after witnessing his father's three marriages, his mother's life put into a desperate tailspin every time he strayed and it made the papers for everyone to see, Ben had no desire to let anyone close. Give anyone that kind of power.

And yet somehow Natalia already had it. She'd infuriated him the night of the engagement party with her sly innuendoes that he was running this camp for his own personal gain. And her suggestion that his family was somehow *beneath* her, what with her own wild-child antics splashed across the papers on a weekly basis.... She'd managed to insult him in the deepest, most personal way possible all in the space of a few minutes. Had she known instinctively that such insults would catch him on the raw? Ben knew he was sensitive about his family. Protective of his mother and sisters. How could he not be, when the press loved to lambast or ridicule them on an almost daily basis? And yet Princess Natalia courted that kind of coverage. The thought made him feel sick. How could a woman like her affect him this way? Make him want so much?

Today her snooty princess routine had also annoyed him, more than it should have, perhaps. He'd expected her time here would take her down a peg or two, not polish her pedestal. He hadn't counted on his staff being wide-eyed and tongue-tied in her presence, or Natalia acting like some kind of Grace Kelly.

Yet even so, he shouldn't be so bothered. He knew it wasn't just Natalia's workplace behaviour that was bothering him. Hell, he'd expected that. He certainly hadn't thought she'd meekly slot herself into the office and be anything close to efficient or productive. He'd thought he'd even enjoy seeing her flounder a bit, watching her get nowhere with her airs and graces.

No, something else was making him hot under the collar, and he knew just what it was. *Desire*. Princess Natalia Santina was a beautiful woman. At the engagement party her charms had been obvious in a tiny, silver spangled dress that barely covered her bottom. He'd taken in those hazel cat's eyes, lithe curves and endless legs and felt an expected kick of lust, easy to dismiss.

Yet today when she'd leaned across his desk and he'd seen the T-shirt stretch across her breasts, when he breathed in the citrusy scent of her perfume, something clean and fresh he hadn't expected, when his gaze was inevitably drawn to her again and again, he felt more than just a normal kick of lust. He felt a deeper twist of longing he wasn't ready to acknowledge, much less feel. When he saw the flash of vulnerability in her eyes, when her pointed quips made him want to smile, when he *enjoyed* her company…he felt that longing inside of him twist harder and start to snap.

Control. He was losing it. He didn't want to want this woman. In any way. He had enough to do arranging this camp, managing his own business and making sure his siblings stayed on a steady course. He didn't need the complication of a woman—any woman, but especially one as dangerously high-profile as Princess Natalia.

Far better to steer clear of her except in the office, or he'd see himself splashed across the tabloids like the rest of his family, and that was the *last* thing he wanted.

Straightening, he pulled a sheaf of papers towards him and determined to work for the rest of the afternoon—and not give the aggravating princess another thought.

He stayed in his office until after seven, immersed in his work. He heard the muted farewells of the others leaving, the sound of the door closing, when he decided to finish up back at the beach house he'd rented for his time on the island. His equilibrium mostly restored, Ben grabbed his attaché and opened his office door, stopping abruptly when he saw Natalia still bent over the filing cabinet.

The first thing he noticed was the way her skirt pulled across the rounded curve of her bottom. Then he jerked his gaze upwards and realised she was still filing away. The thought shocked him, for if she was still here it meant she hadn't been slow on purpose. So what was really going on? Ben had no idea, but this perplexing insight into the woman he wanted to dismiss made him pause. Frown.

She straightened and, seeming to sense his presence, turned. Ben noticed her guarded expression, her eyes veiled before she tilted her head and gave him a flirty smile. That was the expression he was used to seeing, yet it didn't ring true right now.

'You didn't have to stay late.'

Natalia lifted one slender shoulder in a shrug. 'I wanted to get the job done.' She glanced at the remaining few files. 'I've decided I despise filing.'

'It is a bit tedious.'

'That too.' She tucked a strand of wheat-blonde hair behind her ear and turned back to the cabinet.

Ben saw how stiff her shoulders were, her whole body nearly vibrating with tension. She also looked exhausted, and to his own shock he found himself saying, 'Let me finish it.'

'I can do it—' she insisted, surprisingly fierce, but Ben had already slotted the remaining files into the cabinet and closed the drawer. It had taken less than a minute. Why, he wondered, had it taken her hours? Surely even the most incompetent person could manage it quicker than that. Yet looking at her drawn face and shadowed eyes he didn't think it had been some kind of revenge. She'd actually, in her own way, been trying.

'So you finished your first day,' he said lightly. He had come to stand quite close to her in order to finish the filing, and he was conscious of her slender form, the sweep of her satiny cheek, the way her chest rose and fell. He took a step back. 'Congratulations.'

She gave him a sharp look, reminding him, to his relief, of the spoilt princess he'd encountered at the engagement party. 'Much to your disappointment, I'm sure.'

'I wouldn't say that.'

'I would. You made this bet in order to see me fail.' She spoke flatly, without her usually lilting playfulness, and Ben found he missed it.

'I made this bet—' he began, then stopped. Why *had* he insisted she volunteer for him for a month? His own kind of revenge for her being the kind of partying, publicity-seeking princess she was? Or to teach her a lesson? Or something far more dangerous—because he wanted to see her again, wanted to be near her? He didn't like any of the choices.

'Cat got your tongue?' Natalia jibed softly. 'Never mind. One day down, twenty-nine to go.' She turned to fetch her coat but Ben got there first, holding it up for her. 'So I can hang up my own coat but not put it back on?' she mocked, yet he sensed a brittle edge to her tone, to her whole self, that he hadn't heard before. It made him wonder what would happen when that brittle edge cracked. What was underneath?

She slipped her arms into the sleeves and as his fingers brushed her shoulders he felt her twang with awareness, her body as taut as a tightly strung bow. He also felt the answering jolt of lust ricochet through his own body, so strong it took all his self-control to release her.

'Let's call a truce for the evening,' he said, and she turned, close enough to him that her hair brushed his cheek as she moved.

'Are you serious? Where's the fun in that?'

'I'm not sure. But keeping up with you is exhausting, Princess.'

'Of course it is,' she replied tartly. 'I move fast.' She swept past him to the door, and Ben was left wondering if she'd been warning him—or putting herself down. She'd sounded almost bitter.

'Let me buy you a drink,' he suggested, 'since we both survived.' The invitation shocked him. The last thing he wanted was to appear in public with Princess Natalia. The press would go wild photographing them, with all the accompanying gossip and speculation. Exactly the kind of thing he despised.

Except right now all he could think about was what he *wanted*. Natalia stared at him, her eyes wide, moist pink lips parted, and lust jolted him again, as if he'd stuck his finger in an electric socket. Going out with Natalia—even if only for a drink—was surely just as dangerous and foolish a thing to do.

Almost as if she sensed the nature of his thoughts, her eyes flashed fire and she buttoned up her coat. 'I never say no to a drink,' she said, and walked out the door.

CHAPTER FOUR

NATALIA decided to take Ben to a trendy, high-end wine bar near the market square, one of her regular haunts. She could have gone somewhere more discreet, where she wouldn't be noticed, but some childish impulse in her made her choose the more obvious place, although whether she wanted to prove Ben right about her or just annoy him she couldn't say. The moment they arrived the waiter fawned over her, stammering in his nervous haste.

'Princess Natalia! I didn't realise you might be gracing us with your presence tonight. Your usual table?'

She waved a hand airily. 'Thank you, Paulo, but perhaps something in the back this time.' Her usual table was in the front window, perfect for the paparazzi, but she had a feeling Ben would balk at that. She could show *some* consideration. She glanced back at Ben, expecting his eyes to have narrowed and lips thinned in disapproval at her notoriety, but his expression was unreadable. 'They know who I am here,' she explained flippantly, and he arched an eyebrow.

'So it appears.'

The waiter led them to a discreet table in the back, tucked in its own corner, and two more waiters descended on them with bowls of olives and nuts.

Ben took the proffered wine list and scanned it blandly, giving Natalia a chance to study him. She nibbled on a nut—in the end she hadn't actually eaten much of the fabulous lunch and she was starving—and gazed at him from under her lashes.

He really was a most attractive man. His hair, light brown and cut quite short, emphasised the hard planes of his cheek-bones and jaw. Funny how brown hair and blue eyes—both so ordinary—could look so amazing, so assured and mas-culine on this one man. Also amazing was the way her body responded to the whole of his features, her heart rate kicking up so she felt nearly breathless.

He glanced up, caught her staring and gave her an all-too-knowing smile. In the dim light his navy eyes glinted almost blackly. 'Any preference?' he asked, indicating the wine list.

'How about champagne?' Natalia suggested, and from the way his eyes narrowed she knew Ben was thinking of the bottle of wine at lunch.

'Champagne, it is.' No sooner had he closed the wine list than a waiter hurried to serve them. 'A bottle of your best champagne,' Ben said blandly, and Natalia arched an eyebrow.

'Do you know how much that will cost?' she asked after the waiter had left and Ben sat back in his chair, scanning the well-heeled crowd around them.

'In a place like this? I'd say about three thousand euros. But I didn't think you concerned yourself with filthy lucre, Princess.'

'I don't,' she threw back at him. 'But I thought you might. New money and all that.'

'I thought we were calling a truce.'

'And I said there was no fun in that.'

Ben gazed at her, his expression thoughtful, assessing. Uncomfortable. He'd looked at her with compassion when he'd finished the filing for her, and this was just about as bad. Too understanding. Too knowing. Natalia shifted in her seat, recrossed her legs. 'So you're going to bait me and bicker with me for the next month?' he finally asked.

She shrugged, unwilling to admit how exhausting that

sounded. But what other choice did she have? What else did she *do*? She certainly couldn't attempt honesty. Intimacy. She'd tried that once and it had been a complete disaster. Just like it had been for Carlotta, ending up heartbroken and a single mother in the bargain. 'Until it gets old,' she finally told him with an attempt at breeziness.

'And how long will that be, do you think?'

'It depends how much fun you are.'

'I think we have different definitions of fun.'

'I have no doubt about that,' she assured him, and he gave her a small smile.

'So, Princess, what do you do with yourself besides shop and party and play?' There was no real censure to his tone, but Natalia felt it all the same. His choice of words were telling enough. He thought she was shallow. What a surprise. She didn't actually expect him to think any differently, yet his assumption still annoyed her.

'What else is there? Unless you're going to bore me with a lecture about work and duty and the satisfaction of a job well done.' She rolled her eyes, and even though Ben smiled slightly she still sensed his disapproval.

'All right, here's another question. What do *you* hope to gain from this next month?'

Any number of flip answers could have tumbled off her tongue, yet for some reason Natalia remained silent. Ben's question seemed so sincere, she was oddly reluctant to offer another jibe. And, she realised, she wanted to know the answer. Unfortunately she was the one who was meant to give it, and she had no idea.

'Cat got your tongue?' Ben said softly, echoing her earlier words.

'I must admit, I haven't thought about this next month as anything but an endurance test.'

'Fair enough. It's all I pitched it as.'

'But now you're thinking of something else?'

He shrugged, one powerful shoulder lifting. 'Only that it's an awfully long time to just endure.'

She leaned forward with a catlike smile. 'A perfect reason to end the bet right now. We could both walk away.'

He let out a low laugh. 'Oh, I wasn't thinking of anything like that,' he assured her, his gaze lingering and speculative. 'Most definitely not.' The waiter came then with the champagne, popping the cork with a flourish and pouring two glasses of a very expensive vintage. Ben raised his glass in a toast, and Natalia followed suit. 'To the next twenty-nine days,' he said, 'and all they promise.'

Natalia murmured her agreement and took a sip of the champagne, the bubbles crisp on her tongue. What *could* she gain from the month ahead? Ben's question bothered her, not just because she didn't know the answer, but because of what it implied. He made it sound as if this little exercise was meant to teach the spoilt princess a lesson in kindness and compassion, blah, blah, blah. It just showed how lacking Ben thought her in those qualities. And maybe she was. Yet she didn't know how to change—or if she could.

'What's wrong?' he said, and she looked up, startled that he'd sensed the change in her mood.

'What on earth could be wrong?' she replied lightly. 'I'm drinking some of the best champagne I've ever had with a handsome man, even if he is a bit of a stuffed shirt. Maybe a glass or two will loosen him up.' She gave him a flirtatious look from under her lashes, putting their conversation back on familiar territory, firm ground.

'Going on the offensive?' Ben replied drily, startling her again.

'Is that what you call flirting?'

'In your case, yes. You don't like it when I ask questions.'

She couldn't believe how well he understood her. It made her furious, and a bit scared, and more determined than ever to keep it light. 'Or perhaps you just don't like flirting.'

'Oh, I don't mind flirting,' Ben assured her in a lazy drawl that sent unwanted awareness tingling along Natalia's spine and uncoiling deep inside of her. 'But you're not flirting,' he added, taking a sip of champagne. 'You're just trying to keep me from getting to know you.'

She let out an abrupt laugh, the sound sharp and bordering on bitter, and far, far too revealing. 'You don't *want* to get to know me.'

He stilled, his glass halfway raised to his lips. 'Poor little princess?' he mocked gently. 'Nobody understands you? Nobody loves you?'

Natalia stared at him, wanting to laugh it off, *needing* to, yet somehow she couldn't. Her chest felt tight, her throat aching. She took a sip of champagne to ease the soreness. 'Of course,' she finally said lightly. 'Would you really expect anything else from me?'

'I'm not sure,' Ben said slowly, and Natalia jerked her surprised gaze to his own thoughtful one.

'I'm an open book,' she said, raking her hands through her hair and giving him a challenging little smile. 'Obviously.'

'Why did it take you so long to do that filing?' Ben asked quietly, and Natalia stilled, the smile slipping right off her face. For a second she felt horribly exposed, as if he'd just stripped her clothes, or even her skin, right off in the middle of the restaurant. Ben gazed at her with that same thoughtful seriousness, and Natalia scrambled to regain her equanimity. Her armour.

She raised one hand, waggling her fingers. 'Filing is murder on the nails. I wanted to keep my manicure.'

His mouth tightened, although his expression remained thoughtful. Knowing. 'You'll have to say goodbye to your nails next week, when the camp starts. I doubt your manicure will survive on the football pitch.'

'Yes, and just what do you expect me to *do* on a football pitch?'

'Whatever needs doing,' Ben replied. His tone was equable, and yet Natalia sensed that hardness underneath that told her this man was a formidable adversary. He'd managed to get her father to agree to her volunteering for a month; he could probably get anyone to agree to just about anything. In fact, she realised, swallowing drily, he could get her to agree to all manner of things....

She pushed that thought aside, as well as the accompanying images that danced through her mind of Ben looking at her with heavy-lidded languor rather than this quiet speculation. Ben drawing her to him and brushing those soft, mobile lips against her own. Ben slipping his hands...

No. She willed the images and thoughts away. Thinking about getting any closer to Ben Jackson was foolish to the point of insanity. He already guessed—and knew—too much.

'I should tell you,' she informed him blithely, 'I don't know the first thing about football.'

'Oh, don't worry.' His mouth curved into a slow smile. 'I'll teach you.'

Again awareness raced along Natalia's nerve endings and burst like sun-fire through her blood. If she reached one hand out, she would be able to touch him. She wondered how his skin would feel, imagined the rough brush of faint stubble under her fingers. Just how soft would his lips be? She'd spent too much time thinking about his lips, his eyes, the hard, sculpted body underneath that sober silk suit. She needed to stop. Flirting was one thing, desire another. Need, she knew, was dangerous. She'd given into it really only once before and the results had been disastrous and long-lasting. She was still living them down. With the way the press loved to hate her, she always would be.

'I'm not a very good student,' she warned him, keeping her voice as light as ever. That was as close as she could come to admitting the truth.

'Fortunately I'm a good teacher.'

Was she imagining the innuendo, *wanting* it even, or was Ben really suggesting something? His eyes glinted in the candlelight and his mouth quirked upwards. He knew what she was thinking! The realization slammed through Natalia, ignited shock and even fear inside her. How did this man know her so well? She'd spent her whole life trying *not* to be known, even as she inwardly longed for someone to truly understand her, not the pampered party princess, but the girl—and then the woman—underneath…whoever she was. Yet she didn't want the person who truly knew her to be Ben Jackson, with his cynicism and his sneers and his stupid sense of duty. She couldn't.

'I should go,' she said abruptly, the sudden urgency she felt to escape coming through in her tone. Ben quirked one eyebrow.

'It's only a little after eight. The night is young.'

'I have other plans,' Natalia told him, a blatant lie but one she managed with breezy confidence. 'My social calendar is *quite* full, you know.'

He straightened in his seat, his eyes narrowing now not with speculation but, Natalia suspected, with disapproval or even disdain. Well, at least that was more familiar. She stood, and a waiter hurried to her side.

'Your Highness…?'

'My coat, please.'

Ben stood as well. 'I'll drive you home.'

'There's no need. I can text my driver—'

'And bring him out for no good reason? Why do that?' And she heard—or at least thought she heard—a thread of judgement in his voice. She'd do that because she didn't care about other people. She didn't think about them or their needs. She was selfish, shallow, vain—everything the tabloids said she was. Of course.

'Fine.' Natalia glanced at the table, their three-thousand-dollar bottle of champagne only half finished. 'I'll wait for you to settle up.'

'Oh, don't worry, Princess. They know who I am here.' And he strolled past her with a smile, clearly relishing her surprise and discomfort at hearing her own words laughingly parroted back to her.

Snatching her coat from the waiter, silently fuming at the way he always seemed to best her, Natalia followed Ben out to the street. Her heel caught on a tile in the doorway of the restaurant, and as she pitched forward Ben's arm came around her instinctively, supporting her and drawing her to him so her breasts collided with his hard chest, her own arm coming up around his shoulders in an attempt to steady herself. And yet even as she regained her balance her heart tumbled inside her as if she'd just fallen down a whole flight of stairs.

She breathed in the scent of him, woodsy and clean, and felt the lean strength of his body pressed against her own. Her senses exploded to life with longing, and her breath hitched revealingly as she remained half wrapped around him and stars exploded around her.

No, not stars, just the relentless flash of the paparazzi's cameras. A half-dozen of them had been camped outside of the restaurant, waiting for her exit.

Natalia felt Ben's calm, capable hands steady her and then he stepped away, his face expressionless, yet underneath that purposeful blandness she sensed he was now seething with anger. She felt it like the pulse of her own blood, hot and demanding. She'd just given him some major, and undoubtedly unwanted, publicity.

He strode down the street, away from the flashing cameras, and she followed as best she could, hobbling a little bit. The paparazzi hurried after them, shouting questions in both Italian and English.

'Who is your boy toy now, Princess?'

'Give us a kiss!'

Ben strode faster, suddenly turning a corner onto a dark and narrow side street, and breathless Natalia tried to keep up. 'Wait—'

'You want to stay for that?' he asked in a sneer. 'Of course you do. That kind of publicity stunt is right up your alley, Princess.'

So he thought she'd tripped on purpose, for the cameras. It didn't really surprise her, yet it still hurt. 'I just,' she panted, 'want to keep from breaking my ankle. My heel broke when I tripped.'

Ben glanced back at her, then ducked into an alley between two tall and crumbling buildings. Natalia could barely see, and she tripped over some old terracotta pots piled against the wall. They clattered onto the cobbles, the sound echoing off the high walls. She blinked, the darkness pressing close all around her, making her palms damp and her heart thud. She *hated* the dark, especially unlit, enclosed spaces like this wretched alley. 'Where…where are we going?'

'I don't want any more pictures,' Ben growled. 'So if you think this next month is your chance to drag me through the gutter press, think again, Princess.'

She heard the sound of motorcycles speeding off into the distance. 'I think we lost them.' Her voice sounded high and frightened to her own ears, and the thought that Ben might guess how scared she was made her furious. Another thing for him to mock her about. 'Anyway, didn't you say any publicity is good publicity?' she reminded him defiantly.

Ben turned so quickly she nearly lost her balance. He prowled closer, the strength and breadth of him both intimidating and overwhelming in this dark, narrow alley. She'd been scared of the dark; now she was frightened of something else. Or not frightened exactly, but aware. Definitely aware.

The stone wall of the building came up hard against her back, and Ben was so close she had to tilt her head up to look at him. She could barely see his face in the darkness and gloom, but she still felt his anger.

And something else—for whatever was pulsing between them was powerful, dangerous and impossible to resist. He stepped closer, so she could feel the length of his body against her own, heard the thunder of her heart in her ears and the ragged tear of both of their breathing, unnaturally loud in the enclosed space. He dipped his head so his lips hovered above her own. Desire spiralled inside her, crazy and out of control even though he hadn't even kissed her.

But he would...wouldn't he? Her mind was dizzy, overcome by his closeness. All she could think about was the feel of his lips on hers, the *need* of it. Her head fell back, her lips parted in silent, open invitation.

'Don't play games with me, Princess,' Ben breathed, and his lips were so close if she moved at all she would be touching him. *Kissing* him. Yet she didn't move, couldn't, because her body was frozen, paralysed with this helpless yearning. She remained pinned against the wall, her head tilted back, her lips open, her body pulsing with need. She wanted him to move. She wanted him to kiss her.

And he almost did. She felt it in him, that inexorable craving, and knew he was about to cover his mouth with her own. She was already dizzily imagining it, longing for it—and then he stepped away.

His breath came in a ragged rush and Natalia slumped against the wall, her legs as weak and wobbly as a newborn colt's. 'They've gone now,' he said flatly. 'Let's get out of here.'

Silently Natalia followed him out of the dark alley, her body trembling with aftershocks of emotion, her lips stinging as if he'd actually kissed her.

CHAPTER FIVE

'THE Truth Behind Jackson Sports Camps,' Ben read aloud. His staff shifted uneasily in front of him, their eyes downcast. *'Princess Natalia's New Toy Boy,'* he continued, his voice gaining a definite edge. He threw the newspaper down on his desk, the movement one of disgust if not dismissal. He was furious with the press, with Natalia, and most of all with himself for allowing this to happen. His charitable enterprise was being dragged through the mud before the first day of camp. Exactly the kind of thing he avoided at all costs. The kind of tawdry publicity he despised.

Why on earth had he gone out for a drink with Natalia Santina? He'd surely known what the risks were, and yet he'd gone and done it anyway. Recklessly. Stupidly. And he knew why, even if he didn't like the reason.

Because he wanted her.

He wanted her physically, had been so close to kissing her last night he'd almost tasted the sweetness of her lips, better than any champagne they could have drunk. His hands had ached to slide along the lush curves encased in that tight little skirt, slip beneath the snug T-shirt and touch the warm golden skin underneath.

He'd never wanted a woman so much, felt desire so painfully, and yet that wasn't what infuriated him. It was the other, more dangerous wanting. He wanted to believe there was more to her than the shallow, party-going princess. Wanted to trust those glimpses of raw vulnerability and courage. Wanted more.

And there *was* more to her, he thought grimly. She was a vindictive, selfish bitch as well. He'd asked her out for a simple drink, and she'd used the opportunity—and him—shamelessly. He glanced up at his three employees. 'If the press rings, tell them we have no comment and the camp will go ahead as planned. And,' he finished, his voice sharpening, 'when Natalia arrives, tell her to see me immediately.' They nodded, and with a jerk of his head he dismissed them.

Alone in his office Ben took the newspaper and scanned the front page article once more. It was just as infuriating upon the second reading. The Santina family exploits, he saw, took up most of the tabloid's pages. Alessandro and Allegra's engagement took second place to other, more salacious events. Princess Sophia, apparently, had eloped to India with a maharajah. Carlotta, the disgraced single mum, was now in the company of some jilted prince. And Natalia had had the gall to accuse his family of bad behaviour!

He glanced at the photo of him and Natalia in front of the wine bar. It looked all too much like some kind of lovers' embrace. His arm was snugged around her waist, her head upon his shoulder. And the other photo...a carefully angled picture of them standing close together at the restaurant, with the accompanying caption: *Charity Work a Cover for Natalia's Next Conquest?*

Disgust and anger roiled in his stomach and he threw the newspaper down again. She'd planned it all perfectly, and played him for a complete fool.

A light knock sounded on the door, and then Natalia poked her head in, a small smile playing around her mouth, her eyebrows arched. Was she actually *smirking*? Ben rose from his desk.

'Come in,' he said coldly. 'And shut the door behind you.'

'Ooh, somebody didn't sleep well,' Natalia remarked as she closed the door and came to stand in front of his desk.

'You aren't wearing your T-shirt,' Ben said, knowing it was probably the most inane thing he could have said but unable to keep from noticing. She wore a slim black pencil skirt and crisp white blouse, standard office wear, and yet somehow on her it looked as sexy and inappropriate as a black lace negligee. He could not keep his gaze from roving down those endless legs encased in sheer black tights, ending in high black stiletto heels. The skirt emphasised the perfect curve of her hip and thigh, and she'd left the white blouse unbuttoned at the throat, a silver pendant nestling in the shadowy, golden V between her breasts.

'I had to have it washed,' Natalia told him. 'So if it really is required uniform, perhaps you could find a spare?'

He nodded tersely, not wanting to dwell on it or how enticing she looked in the clothes she'd chosen to wear. He shouldn't have brought it up in the first place. 'Tell me, Natalia, how is it that in twenty-four hours you've managed to put this entire enterprise into complete disarray?'

'Natural talent, I suppose.'

Ben planted his fists on his desk and leaned forward. 'Do you realise,' he demanded, 'how much harm your stupid little ploy has caused?'

Natalia blinked, surprise flashing across her features at the restrained fury in his tone. Then her face cleared of all expression except perhaps boredom. 'Which stupid little ploy,' she drawled, 'are you referring to?'

'You didn't read the papers this morning?'

'I make a point never to look at them.'

'How surprising. I would have thought you'd enjoy such an exercise.'

'Just more proof of how little you know me.'

'What I know,' Ben gritted, 'is your little plan to take my employees out to lunch and then trip all over me worked admirably. The press have sunk their teeth into the story and are claiming the only reason I'm sponsoring this sports camp is as a cover to get into your bed.'

'How ridiculous,' she scoffed. 'Surely there's an easier way to get into my bed.'

For a split second Ben once again had the bizarre sense that she was putting herself down on purpose, and he felt his anger drain away. He realized he was overreacting, and he knew it was because of his own experiences with the press. Still he could not get the bitter taste out of his mouth, the sickening feeling of being used and manipulated simply for the sake of a photograph. 'Read that,' he said, thrusting a paper into her hands.

She took it, glancing down at it without seeming to really read it. After a few seconds she tossed it back onto the desk. 'All of it drivel. Just ignore it. It's just a trashy tabloid anyway.'

'Did you *read* it?' Ben demanded, and she blinked.

'I scanned it.'

'Did you see the accusations they were making against the camp?'

She lifted one slender shoulder in an aggravatingly dismissive shrug. 'It's just gossip.'

'Which you obviously don't care about,' Ben snapped, 'based on how heavily you're featured in these rags. I know you court the tabloids, Princess. You make sure they get all the photos they want of you at all your high-flying parties.' She said nothing, only lifted her chin in challenge, which infuriated him all the more. 'I read an astonishingly thorough exposé of an affair you had with some Frenchman,' he drawled, 'including rather intimate details you were clearly happy to provide.'

She stilled, and Ben had an odd sense that she'd somehow retreated from him even though she hadn't moved. 'You've really done your research, Ben,' she said with a cool little smile. 'I'm so impressed.'

'Trust me, it didn't take much. Just pick up a paper.'

'You've made your point.'

Ben sighed, raking a hand through his hair. 'My point, Natalia, is that I run a respectable business, with sensitive, high-profile clients who come to me for discreet financial advice. This kind of exposure is exactly what I don't want and can't have.'

'Then maybe you shouldn't have asked me to volunteer.'

'Maybe I shouldn't have,' Ben agreed. He'd thought he could handle the press, handle her, but right now he felt like he couldn't. He felt like he was spinning out of control, and not just because of the press. Because of her.

'So,' Natalia said, 'is that it? You lasted one day with me?'

'Not a chance, Princess. I never lose a bet.'

'Just your temper.'

He glanced down at the papers again, felt a stirring of regret. 'I'm sorry. I shouldn't have become so angry.'

'You must be used to this kind of thing,' Natalia said, gesturing to the paper. 'Your family is always featured in the tabloids back in England.' He knew it all too well. 'I've worked very hard to make sure *I'm* not featured in—'

'Which is exactly why you're so annoyed that you got dragged in this time,' she finished curtly. 'Shall I shed a tear? Now you know how it feels.'

He'd been dragged in before, and he hated it, but he wasn't about to tell Natalia that. 'Are you saying you don't go after that kind of publicity? That you're *innocent*?'

'Is that so hard to believe?'

'You know your own history—'

'Better than you do.'

'You're saying none of what the tabloids print is true?' Ben demanded. He watched her flush, and with a jolt of regret he realised he'd hurt her.

'Not all of it is true,' she said stiffly. 'And in this instance, no, I didn't plan it all. Really, you give me far too much credit. I took everyone out to lunch yesterday to be *nice*. End of story. And when we were coming out of the wine bar I tripped. You saw my broken heel yourself. The press jumped all over it as they always do, and they made it look as naughty as they could.' Her lush lips curved in a brittle smile. 'Really, I wouldn't expect anything less.'

Ben stared at her. Even though she was effecting a careless, relaxed pose, he suspected that's all it was. A pose. He sensed a deeper, darker sea of emotions churning underneath. Disappointment. Hurt. Fear. Anger too—and he didn't know if it was directed at him, the press or maybe even the whole world. If she hated the tabloid coverage, he wondered, why on earth did she go out of her way to get it? Granting interviews. Posing for photos. Waving at the cameras. He'd assumed she enjoyed the notoriety.

Now he wondered. Was Natalia just pretending—and why? It was a question he didn't really feel like examining…or answering.

He straightened, raking his hands through his hair before dropping them to his sides. 'I'm sorry,' he said quietly. 'I see now that I overreacted a bit because I hate the press.'

'You hate the press?' She widened her eyes in mocking astonishment. 'What a surprise.'

'Shocking, I know—'

'Did something happen,' Natalia asked abruptly, 'to make you hate it so much? Something specific?'

Ben pressed his lips together. He had no desire to trot out his little sob stories, his mother's distress at having her private heartache made into public shame, how the press had pounced on his own weaknesses again and again to milk a story. 'I simply find the entire practice of making money off people's anguish completely reprehensible.' He stopped himself from saying anything more, for he knew he'd already revealed too much. *Anguish*. Yes, that's what his mother had felt. What he had felt. Yet he didn't want Natalia to know. 'I suspect having you volunteer here has challenged me as much as it has you.'

'As long as we're both getting something out of it.'

'When I asked you to volunteer,' he continued steadily, 'I didn't foresee this kind of press coverage.' That wasn't, he knew, quite true. He had anticipated something like it, but he'd willfully ignored it, told himself he could handle it. And right now it felt like he couldn't. 'That was foolish on my part, I realise.'

Natalia's eyes flashed, this time with sudden humour. 'Wait a minute. You *asked* me?'

Ben felt a flicker of admiration for the way she adjusted, always matching him. And a flicker of something else. He watched her chest rise and fall under that crisp white blouse and he wanted to undo its buttons. 'Didn't I ask?' he said, feigning confused innocence. 'And you so politely agreed?' A wry smile tugged at his mouth, and she smiled back, the moment spinning on and turning into something else—something that reminded Ben of how slender and lithe her body had felt last night, how close his lips had been to hers. How much he'd wanted to kiss her.

'I think you're rewriting history as much as the press do,' she said.

Which brought them back to their current situation with an unwelcome thud. Ben jerked his gaze away from her blouse and those tempting little buttons. 'I'm sorry for losing my temper and accusing you unfairly,' Ben said. 'I shouldn't have jumped to conclusions. But we can't have this,' he continued, glancing down at the newspapers. 'If the camp receives negative local press before it even starts, it could affect parents' decisions to send their children, not to mention some of the camp's endorsements.' He glanced up, saw she looked serious now too, and maybe even a little sad. 'I know you think I'm doing this as some sort of PR stunt—'

'I don't really,' she said quietly.

'The truth is,' Ben said, the words sounding and feeling awkward, 'I'm doing it for the children. Well, myself and the children. I—I used to love playing sport. It gave me a great sense of confidence and—and control when I needed it most, and I want to share that with others, with children who might never have an opportunity to kick a football or run around the pitch.' He gave a small laugh, feeling oddly vulnerable at having shared so much. He knew to her it must sound like a small thing, but it felt like his very soul.

'I understand,' Natalia assured him with one of her lightning smiles. 'The next time you ask me out for a drink, I'll say no.'

He let out a little laugh. Natalia never let up, never admitted defeat. He liked that, he realised. Once again he wondered about the woman underneath the party-princess, publicity-seeking facade. Was she there? Was she real? And did he want her to be? 'All right,' he said at last. 'Fair enough. Now we really ought to do some proper work. I'm sure Francesca has some more photocopying or filing for you to do.'

'Right,' Natalia said. Her tone had turned brittle again, all traces of that odd moment of intimacy vanished. 'I'm on the job,' she said, giving him a mock salute, and left the room with Ben still staring after her, wondering if he'd ever understand her…and why he wanted to.

Frowning, he glanced at the papers again, and saw a few inches of print he hadn't noticed before. *Jackson's Prodigal Daughter Parties with the Earl?*

His frown deepened as he pulled the papers towards him and scanned the few lines. Apparently his stepsister Angel Tilson had left the engagement party last weekend with the Earl of Pemberton. Ben didn't know him, but from the blurry photograph he looked dark, menacing, and rich. What could Angel possibly be up to this time?

Still frowning, he reached for his mobile and punched in his sister's number. Although he wasn't related by blood to Angel, his father's second wife's daughter from a previous relationship, he still felt responsible for her. Ben knew Angel had never really felt part of the boisterous Jackson clan. Tough and street-wise, she'd always been determined to make it on her own.

She answered the phone after several rings. 'Big brother,' she greeted him in a drawl, 'what new worry has you ringing me?'

Ben smiled in spite of his concern. Angel knew him well. *So did Natalia.* Pushing that uncomfortable thought aside, he glanced at the paper in front of him. 'What are you doing with the Earl of Pemberton, Angel?'

'Having a blast,' she told him, 'of course. Had your daily dose of the tabloids, Ben? Why don't you just stop reading those rags?'

'Because I like to know what's going on in my own family.'

'Don't worry about me.'

'You know I do.'

She sighed, and the sad sound pulled at Ben's heart. He knew many were quick to assume Angel was just like her mother, social-climbing or even money-grubbing. Few tried to see beneath her streetwise facade, but Ben thought he did. He tried to know the woman underneath all the wisecracks, because he sensed she was both courageous and vulnerable.

Just like Natalia.

Why couldn't he stop thinking about her?

'Be careful, Angel.'

'I always am.'

'I mean it. I don't even know this guy—'

'He's rich and titled, Ben. What more could I want?'

'Don't sell yourself short.'

She said nothing, and yet that silence seemed so lonely. So sorrowful. Ben sighed. 'You will ring me if you need anything? Ever?'

'Of course.' But he could tell she didn't mean it.

After saying goodbye, he disconnected the call and stared into space, thinking once again of another sharp, funny woman who hid her true self from him.

Back in the front office Natalia drew in a big breath and let it out slowly. Right. Photocopying. Filing. She could do this. She smiled at Francesca.

'You have something for me to do?'

'It's rather boring—'

'I think the point of me being here is to *do* boring,' Natalia said drily, and listened as Francesca directed her to a pile of about a zillion envelopes that all needed stuffing with some sort of support letter. Perfect. It would take several hours, and required no more skill than putting one piece of paper inside another. She *could* do this. She nearly sagged with relief.

Yet Natalia soon found that stuffing envelopes left her mind all too free to wander. And to wonder. Did Ben now believe she hadn't planned to trip into his arms on purpose? As pleasant as it had been to feel his hard body against her own, it had still been completely unintentional. And then in that dark alley... Just remembering that exquisitely taut moment caused a shudder of longing to ripple through her. He'd been so close to kissing her. A single breath away. He'd been *going* to kiss her, and then he'd forced himself to stop.

That was why he was so angry today, Natalia decided as she sealed yet another envelope. He'd desired her last night, and he knew she knew it, and it annoyed him. She could just imagine how aggravated Ben Jackson would be at wanting someone he thought shallow, spoilt and completely inappropriate.

She wondered just what kind of women decorated his

arm…and warmed his bed. Brisk and business-minded, like himself? Surely not. She could certainly see Ben entertaining a model or starlet, and then calmly discarding them when he'd finished with their services. Sex—or even love—was probably just another item to tick on his to-do list.

She pressed her lips together and tossed another sealed envelope onto her growing stack. She would not be one of his ticked boxes. She would not be used by Ben Jackson at all. She might have a well-earned wild reputation, but she stayed in charge. In control. And if Ben thought *he* was determined to resist her…he had no idea how determined she could be. She wouldn't get close to anyone, and certainly not Ben Jackson.

The rest of the week passed without incident. The press was thankfully occupied with the exploits of other members of the Santina family, and tailing Natalia being driven to work every day was not noteworthy enough to make a headline. Ben was out of the office for two days, checking out the island's stadium where the camp would be launched on Monday. Natalia hadn't given too much thought to her duties after this week, but as she helped Francesca sort stacks of youth-size T-shirts she wondered just what Ben was going to have her *do* on a football pitch. She could barely kick a ball; she'd never been much of one for sport. School, as a whole, had simply been something to endure.

Late Friday afternoon Ben strolled into the office, looking remarkably refreshed and energised. Natalia, in comparison, felt about as refreshed as a wet towel. Working just one week had very nearly done her in.

'So, Princess,' he said. 'Be ready to work hard on Monday.'

Natalia glanced pointedly at the stack of T-shirts she'd been going through with Francesca. 'Oh, excuse me, this isn't working hard?'

His faint smile turned into a full-fledged grin. 'Not even close. On Monday you'll be working up a sweat.'

'Didn't anyone ever tell you that women *glow*?'

'Then on Monday you'll be fluorescent.'

'What a thought.' She shook her head and refolded a T-shirt. 'You're enjoying this, aren't you?' she said, without rancor. Something about Ben's blatant enthusiasm was almost catching.

'I'm looking forward to starting the camp,' Ben admitted. 'Getting out on the pitch.'

'You said you played yourself?'

'A long time ago.'

'Most millionaires would just throw a pile of money at a charity,' Natalia said thoughtfully, 'not get as involved as you do.'

For a second Ben looked almost trapped by her question, as if she'd asked something embarrassingly personal. Perhaps she had. Then he shrugged and said, 'I like to be out there, actually playing. Coaching. It's fun for me.'

'Now, *fun* is not a word I'd associate with you.'

He slid her a sudden, sideways grin that ignited her senses. 'You don't know me well enough to say that, Princess.'

'Oh, really?'

'Really. And wait until I get you out onto the pitch. We're both going to have a *lot* of fun.'

She grimaced. 'That sounds like a threat.'

'Consider it a promise,' he told her, and she arched her eyebrows.

Was he flirting? It felt like flirting.

'If we're going to have so much of your kind of fun on the pitch,' she said, 'perhaps we should have my kind of fun before.' As soon as she spoke the words, she realized how provocative they sounded—almost as if she were propositioning him. Still she smiled in challenge, refused to avert her gaze as Ben stared at her speculatively, one shoulder propped against the doorway of his office.

'That sounds…intriguing.'

Natalia's heart rate kicked up a notch. *Didn't it just.* 'How about a deal?' she suggested. 'I'll experience your kind of fun at camp, and you have to experience my kind of fun this weekend. Going out,' she clarified quickly, and felt herself blush as she considered what he might have thought she meant.

'Out where?'

'I get to pick. It'll be a surprise.'

'And why should I do this?' Ben inquired in a silky voice. 'I don't need to make a deal, princess. You're already here because I convinced your father.'

'Do it,' Natalia told him, 'because you want to.' Ben's gaze blazed into her own and distantly she wondered what on earth she was doing, daring him like this. *Wanting* him like this. And he knew it. And maybe even wanted her too. It was crazy, scary, and yet she couldn't keep herself from it, from *him*, like a child playing with matches. Someone was going to get burned.

'All right,' Ben said softly. 'When?'

'Tomorrow.'

'Where?'

Natalia drew a steadying breath. How had this even happened? How had they got to this place? 'You can pick me up at the palazzo at noon.'

Ben was still gazing at her, his expression narrowed and assessing, and Natalia had the strange feeling that he was as surprised as she was that he'd agreed. That they were going out…tomorrow. Finally he nodded, and Natalia managed an insouciant smile despite the thud of her heart and the sickness of her palms. 'Wear something nice. And don't expect to be home until late.'

'Sounds like you've already got a plan.'

'Maybe.' She didn't, not really, not beyond showing Ben what fun could really mean. And it had nothing to do with football pitches. For a second, she dizzily imagined just how much *fun* the two of them could have. And then swallowed audibly.

Ben's gaze still rested on her, considering, heavy, and once more Natalia wondered just what on earth she was doing. Risking. Then, without another word, the tension still tautening the air between them, he turned and went into the office.

As he closed the door Natalia sagged, saw she'd been clenching the T-shirt she'd been folding so hard there were nail marks in the fabric.

When Natalia arrived back at the palazzo that evening, her mind still buzzing from her exchange with Ben, her mother called her into her private rooms and Natalia knew from the lavender silk evening gown her mother wore that once again royal duty beckoned.

'Back from your charity work?' Zoe asked, which Natalia knew was how her mother liked to view her volunteering for Ben Jackson. She nodded, and Zoe turned to a waiting maid. 'I'll wear the amethyst parure.'

'Very good, Your Highness.' The maid went to fetch the magnificent set of diamond and amethyst earrings, necklace, bracelet cuffs and tiara from her mother's private safe. Zoe turned to Natalia.

'We have several foreign dignitaries coming to dine tonight. You will attend. It is perfectly possible that one may represent your future husband.'

Natalia felt an icy plunging sensation in her middle. 'My engagement to Prince Michel only ended a few weeks ago.'

'All the more reason to press on. You are twenty-seven years old, Natalia. High time you were married.'

'It's the twenty-first century, Mother,' Natalia protested, even though she'd made this argument before, to little effect. 'Twenty-seven could be considered young these days.'

'Not for a princess,' Zoe replied firmly. 'In any case, we are not ruled by current fashions. Your marriage is an important negotiation that will strengthen our country.'

'Plenty of royals marry whomever they please,' Natalia pointed out, and Queen Zoe arched her eyebrows.

'You do not, I trust,' she said, 'have anyone in mind.'

Ridiculously and unreasonably, Ben—his quirking smile, his powerful body—flashed through her mind. 'Of course not.'

Zoe sighed. 'I know it is hard for a young woman to face her royal duty. And perhaps your father and I have been too lenient, allowing you the freedom to live life as you saw fit for too long.' Although her mother spoke delicately, Natalia still heard the judgment, felt it in herself. She hadn't done much with her life. She knew that. She just didn't know how to change, or if she even wanted to. What was the point?

The maid returned with the parure and laid out the pieces on her mother's vanity. Zoe glanced down at them, her eyes narrowed in assessment. 'It is time you stepped into the role to which you were born, Natalia. It is time you started acting like a princess.' The maid lowered the bejewelled tiara onto Zoe's silver hair. Her mother met Natalia's gaze in the ornate mirror. Natalia saw compassion there, but also an implacable will she knew she didn't have the strength or resources to defy. 'You will start,' Queen Zoe told her, 'tonight.'

An hour later, dressed in a sedate and modest evening gown of ivory silk, Natalia followed her mother into the palazzo's formal receiving room. She hated these evenings. Hated how she felt like a dressed-up doll, or worse, a slab of meat. Something to be assessed and bargained over, and then picked apart or even devoured.

The hours dragged on as her parents engaged the dignitaries in social niceties and political innuendoes that Natalia didn't even bother to listen to. She'd long ago learned not to have an opinion about any of it. As they headed into the dining room, her mother whispered in her ear once more.

'At least smile, Natalia. You're behaving like a block of wood.'

'I thought that was exactly what you wanted,' Natalia muttered.

Her mother silenced her with a quelling look and swept into the dining room. Natalia took her place at the table, her mind wandering as the conversation continued to flow around her. Then she heard her name.

'The Princess Natalia has enjoyed herself, hasn't she?' One of the dignitaries—from some Middle Eastern island nation, Natalia thought—glanced at her with a smile, although his words had held a sharp edge.

'All young girls enjoy themselves,' Zoe answered with a gracious smile. 'But the princess now needs a strong husband to guide her.'

Natalia nearly choked on her vichyssoise. She didn't want a man to guide her. Or even love her. She didn't want to get married at all. The thought of being auctioned off to some nameless autocratic royal made her insides clench in a spasm of both fear and fury.

Even as she told herself that her parents couldn't *force* her to marry anyone, she acknowledged that they very well could. They could certainly make her life unpleasant or even unbearable unless she agreed to whichever husband they had chosen for her. She might as well live in the Middle Ages.

Perhaps she would have been better off with Prince Michel.

'The princess is involving herself with some charity work,' Zoe continued. 'For disadvantaged children.' She turned to Natalia, acknowledging her presence for the first time. 'You find it very rewarding, don't you, my dear?'

Natalia thought of the hundreds of envelopes she'd stuffed and sealed over the past few days. From somewhere she dredged up a small smile. 'Very.'

Zoe smiled at the men assembled, who looked satisfied by Natalia's meek answer. One of them gave her what she suspected he thought was a benevolent look. 'I'm glad to hear the princess is changing her ways.'

'The princess,' Natalia said before she could stop herself, 'is right here.'

The ensuing silence was like a thunderclap. Defiantly Natalia reached for her wine glass and took a large sip. What could they do to her after all? She was twenty-seven years old, a grown woman...

A woman who was dependent on her parents and their generosity because there was no way she could ever support herself. No way she could ever make it in this world.

After an icy pause her mother resumed the conversation, steering it towards more innocuous matters. At the end of the meal Queen Zoe rose to retire with Natalia to one of the smaller salons while the men discussed politics—and her possible marriage—in another room.

As soon as they were alone, the staff dismissed, Zoe turned to Natalia. 'How dare you embarrass me,' she hissed. 'And yourself, and your family. We have been very patient, Natalia. Very tolerant—'

Natalia flushed. 'I didn't like them talking about me as if I wasn't there.'

'That is how it is done, Natalia! That is how these negotiations take place. These men want to see you and how you comport yourself so they can make a report to their sovereign. Is even this concept too difficult for you?'

'I am not,' Natalia said through gritted teeth, 'that stupid.'

'You could have fooled me tonight,' Zoe snapped. 'The way you have carried on these past years, never mind your abysmal performance in school! At least your sisters have learned how to behave themselves.'

That stung. 'Oh, really? Carlotta is unmarried with a child and Sophia eloped with—'

'Their marriages are now settled,' Zoe cut across her, 'and so must yours be.'

'And if I don't want to marry?' Natalia flung out. 'At all?'

Zoe sighed, the anger seeming to drain out of her. 'You are a princess, Natalia. Princesses marry.'

'This is the—'

'Twenty-first century. Yes, I'm well aware.' Her mother sat on a little antique chair, her back ramrod straight as always, and yet for the first time Natalia realised how old her mother looked. Living a life for duty's sake took its toll on you, she supposed. Had her mother ever been happy? Or was happiness not even a consideration?

'What other option do you have, Natalia?' Zoe asked wearily. 'Would you prefer to live your whole life in your parents' palazzo, and then with your brother and his bride, an object of pity and scorn?'

Natalia swallowed. It sounded horrible. *Everything* did. 'I don't want to marry a man who—'

'Doesn't love you?' Zoe filled in, her voice ending on a sigh. 'Really, Natalia, love is for fairy tales.'

'I don't care about love,' Natalia said stiffly. She'd seen and done enough not to trust such a concept. 'I just want respect.'

'Then perhaps you should start acting like you're worthy of it.'

The words felt like a slap. She *knew* she hadn't done much with her life. She didn't have much to be proud of. She'd always known that. She just didn't know how to change. If she could. Even if she wanted to. 'Is that all?' she asked her mother, her voice wooden. 'Because I've had a long day and I'd like to go to bed.'

'Very well.' Zoe sighed and waved her away. 'At least you have curtailed your evening exploits. But I do not want this ridiculous volunteering of yours to interfere with your real duty—and that is to find a husband.'

'Father insisted I volunteer for a month,' Natalia reminded her mother. 'I must do as he says.'

'So you must. And then you must do as I say, Natalia, and marry.'

Nodding again, her heart like a stone inside her, Natalia slipped out of the salon and up the stairs. A week ago volunteering for Ben had seemed like a prison sentence. Now it felt like a reprieve.

CHAPTER SIX

At precisely noon the next day Natalia watched Ben's silver Mercedes pull up in front of the palazzo. She was already waiting in the front foyer, having cleared his entrance with the royal security. Now she checked her reflection in one of the ornate gilt mirrors that lined the hall and attempted to subdue the wild beating of her heart. She was far too excited by the prospect of a day with Ben Jackson, and not a photocopier or football pitch in sight.

'Princess.' Ben's mouth curved in a smile as his gaze swept over her like a wave of sun-warmed water. 'You look delightful.'

'Thank you.' Ben didn't look too bad himself. He wore a lightweight linen suit, his Aviator sunglasses emphasizing the chiselled planes of his face. He opened the passenger door and Natalia slid inside his car, smoothing the cream silk of her designer shift across her thighs.

Ben returned to the driver's seat and as they pulled out of the palazzo's drive he slid her a sideways glance. 'Is that a hat?'

Laughing a little, Natalia reached up to pat the tan feather and silk creation perched pertly on one side of her head. 'Technically it's a fascinator.'

'A what?'

'A fascinator. A millinery creation that is, of course, meant to fascinate.' She smiled at him, enjoying the way his mouth curved in an answering smile, one hand on the steering wheel, the other stretched out along the back of the seat, his fingers nearly brushing her shoulder. Her heart beat hard again and her senses sang in answer to that smile. Natalia knew she was going to enjoy every minute of this day, a day out of time and reality, a day that could actually be a date. She had no doubt that come Monday, she would be no more than Ben's irritating employee—or *volunteer*—once more.

'So I can drive around the island,' Ben told her as he made his way through Santa Maria's capital city, 'but I assume with that outfit you have some destination in mind?'

'As a matter of fact, yes. The island's race course.'

'We're going to a race?'

'A horse race, yes, although admittedly not a hugely important one. I think it's a qualifying race for the derby later this year. But since you seem to be a betting man…'

'I see. And what should we bet on this time, do you think?'

Natalia titled her head, gave him a playful smile. '*We're* betting?'

'Of course, Princess. It's no fun if you don't bet. I don't want to win *money*.'

Her heart was beating so hard and fast she felt it like thunder in her ears. Attempting insouciance was proving harder and harder. 'So what would you like to bet on, then?' she finally asked when she trusted her voice, if not herself. This man was dangerous. And she was dangerous when she was with him. She had no idea what she might give into.

'We'll just have to see,' Ben murmured, and followed her directions to the other side of the island and Santa Maria's race course.

The royal box overlooking the course was empty save for them; since it wasn't a major race her parents and siblings had found other things to occupy them. Natalia slid into her seat and glanced at the line-up of horses racing. 'Apparently,' she told Ben, 'Autumn Nights is the favourite.'

Ben lounged in his seat, flicking through the program with long, lean fingers. 'Then we can't bet on that one.'

'Why not?'

He gave her a lazy smile. 'Neither of us is a sure thing, Princess.'

Natalia glanced down at the program, willed herself not to flush. She had a feeling Ben was not talking about horses. 'Evening Star is considered the underdog,' she said. 'It's his first race. I'll bet on him.'

'To win?'

She nodded. 'And what about you?'

He flicked another glance at the line-up. 'Wild Wishes.'

She had a few of those. Swallowing, Natalia said, 'We still haven't decided just what we're betting on.'

'Well,' Ben said, his voice dropping to a husky murmur, 'I think we should make it interesting.'

She shifted in her seat. 'How interesting?'

'If Evening Star wins, you get to kiss me.'

Desire ran through her like a trail of dynamite, exploding inside of her. 'And if Wild Wishes wins?'

'I get to kiss you.'

Natalia let out a little laugh. 'But that's the same thing.'

'No,' Ben clarified silkily, 'it's not. It's all about who controls the kiss.'

Control. Of course this was about control. Natalia turned away, focusing on the race course beneath them. She fanned herself with her program, and heard Ben chuckle softly.

'Hot, Princess?'

'Wild Wishes is a long shot too,' she informed him, ignoring his little innuendo. 'It might be that neither of us gets a kiss today.'

Ben leaned back in his seat. 'And that,' he said softly, 'would be a pity.'

Yes, it would. Already Natalia was imagining how his lips would feel on hers, hard and demanding. But if *she* controlled the kiss…she felt as if she'd swallowed fireworks, everything fizzing inside her. She didn't know which of them she wanted to win.

The race started, and with it Natalia felt another surge of adrenalin. She felt a fully male energy radiating from Ben's powerful form as he leaned forward to watch the race. Autumn Nights started out in front, but a quarter of the way through the course Wild Wishes pulled ahead.

'Ah-ha,' Ben said softly, and Natalia gave him a knowing smile.

'Evening Star is known to save the best for last.'

'You want to win, Princess?'

'Of course.'

He smiled, and Natalia smiled back, their gazes locking in steely and heated challenge. Natalia had never felt so aware, so alive, or so wanted. After a tense moment she forced herself to turn back to the race.

'Ah-*ha*,' she echoed. 'Look at Evening Star.'

Sure enough Evening Star had pulled a length ahead of Wild Wishes. They watched for several taut moments as the horses galloped, only half a length between them, dust flying from their hooves. Evening Star was still ahead, and Natalia was already envisioning turning to Ben with a little smile, yanking him over to her by his tie and pulling his mouth down to hers…

Then, out of seemingly nowhere, Autumn Nights pulled ahead of both the horses, crossing the finish line a full two lengths in front of Evening Star.

Around them the crowd burst into cheers at such a close victory, and Natalia sank back in her seat, conscious of the swamping sense of disappointment she felt.

'Well,' Ben said with a surprisingly shaky laugh, 'it looks like we both lost.'

'Yes.' Her throat felt absurdly tight. It was just a race; it would have been just a kiss. Yet she felt as if she'd lost out on something wonderful and precious. 'At least there's champagne,' she said lightly, and beckoned a waiter forward to serve them.

The tension between them lessened as they chatted over champagne and strawberries. Natalia forced the thought—and hope—of the kiss back, knowing there was no good dwelling on it now. The moment had passed. Ben would have kissed her for a bet, she realized with a trace of bitterness, but not just to kiss her. Not the way she really wanted to be kissed.

'Why the frown, Princess?'

She glanced up at him, saw his eyes narrowed in that speculative way she'd come to recognize, and gave him an easy smile. 'No reason.'

'Not pining over Evening Star, are you?'

'That,' Natalia told him sweetly, 'would be quite a wild wish.'

He chuckled and leaned back in his seat. 'So do you go to the races often?'

'Occasionally. A royal presence is often required. My father owns one of the horses in this race.'

'Which one?'

'Abdul Akbar. He came in fifth.'

'Too bad.' She just shrugged. 'Are you close to your parents?'

'Close?' Natalia took a sip of champagne, unnerved by the question. 'Are you?' she asked.

'Nope, not going to answer that one. I asked you first.'

'Then I suppose the short answer is no, not really.'

'What's the long answer?'

She stared at him. 'Why do you want to know?'

'Well, Princess,' Ben told her, leaning forward so the male scent of him, aftershave and champagne and even a little bit of strawberry, washed over her, 'it's called making conversation.'

She gave him a tiny smile. 'A talent I didn't think you were capable of.'

'I am, on occasion.'

'So what's the occasion?'

He held his champagne flute aloft. 'Isn't it obvious?'

It had been more comfortable, Natalia thought, when they had been bantering and betting on a kiss. This question—this *conversation*—felt far more intimate and dangerous than a mere brushing of lips ever could have been. 'My parents put the kingdom before their family,' Natalia finally said. 'In many different ways. It created a distance.'

'Duty before love?'

'Something like that.' She really didn't feel like going into it, or remembering the years of secrecy and shame. *Keep it quiet, Natalia. Don't let anyone know how slow you are.* She smiled, took a sip of her drink. 'What about you?'

'Am I close to my parents?' Ben shrugged. 'My father likes to think we're close, but I'm not sure we really are. And I feel very protective of my mother. She's been through too much already.' He pressed his lips together, clearly as uncomfortable as she was revealing anything personal, and Natalia laughed softly.

'You shouldn't have asked the question, Ben, if you weren't willing to answer it.'

He acknowledged her point with a wry half-smile. 'True. Maybe we should stick to talking about films or books. Read anything good lately?'

Definitely not. 'Nope,' Natalia said lightly. She reached for a strawberry and tried to ignore the ache in her chest that radiated outwards, seeming to take over her whole body with its pain. Why, she wondered, did it hurt to have secrets when the thought of them being revealed was so terrifying? Either way she couldn't win.

'So what's next on your agenda for today?' Ben asked, and

Natalia felt a flicker of relief as well as disappointment that the conversation was moving on.

'Dinner at a very nice restaurant on the beach, and then dancing at the island's best club.' She arched her eyebrows. 'Do you dance?'

'Fabulously.'

'Brilliant.'

She rose and Ben followed suit, holding out his hand to escort her from the royal box. After a slight hesitation Natalia took it, needing to feel his fingers wrapped over hers, skin against skin even in just this small way. She knew that even though she had set the schedule for the day, Ben was the one who was in control. How could she doubt it for a moment? He was man who thrived on control, who craved it…and she, Natalia acknowledged with a whisper of panic, could not resist him.

They ate fish caught that afternoon with the waves lapping the shore only a few meters away, and Natalia found herself relaxing, reveling in Ben's attention and interest. He asked her about her life as a princess without sounding snide or condemning, but as if he really wanted to know. And Natalia reeled him with tales of her upbringing, finding moments and anecdotes that had not been tainted by disapproval or duty. She also liked hearing about Ben's climb to his current position as CEO of his own multi-million pound finance management firm, learning more about the man she was finding to be far more fascinating than she'd ever expected.

The sun sunk towards the sea turning its surface to burnishing gold, and they lounged in their chairs, finishing the bottle of wine, the spring air a warm caress.

'So,' Ben finally said, his face in half-shadow, 'dancing.'

'I can't wait to see you dance,' Natalia said, although more than half of her wanted to stay here, in this twilit intimacy and savour simply being alone with Ben. Yet surely that was too dangerous. Better to be in a public place, with other people, where her body—and heart—wouldn't lead her astray.

'And I can't wait to dance with you,' Ben replied, and he signalled for the cheque.

The club Natalia chose was packed with writhing bodies, flashing with strobe lights, and pulsing with music so loud Ben could feel it reverberate through his chest. Perfect. He couldn't get close to Natalia in a place like this, couldn't see the golden glints in her eyes when she laughed, couldn't feel his self-control start to fray as he reached for her again, finding any excuse to touch her. His hand on the small of her back, his arm across the seat of his car, his fingers brushing hers as they clinked glasses. Any excuse at all, even a ridiculous bet on a race horse.

He'd never wanted a woman so much. A woman he knew to be dangerous, inappropriate, *impossible*. He should never be interested in someone like Natalia.

Someone like Natalia. Yet who was she? The partying, publicity-seeking princess, or the woman who laughed and flirted even as he saw the shadow of vulnerability in her eyes? The woman he despised for everything she represented and *was*—spoiled, shallow, vain—or the woman he couldn't get enough of, both emotionally and physically, so he sought her out again and again?

She turned to him now, a flicker of uncertainty in her eyes before she gave him her usual challenging little smile. 'Ready to dance?'

'Of course.'

She'd taken off her ridiculous little hat and fitted jacket, so she wore only a cream silk sheath that lovingly hugged her slender curves. Ben watched her wind her way onto the dance floor with a kick of lust, and then he eyed the heaving crowds with definite reluctance. Yet surely it was better than remaining in the seductive darkness of the restaurant's terrace, listening to the throaty sound of her laughter, watching the setting sun touch her skin with gold. Just enjoying *being* with her, more than with any other woman he'd ever known.

No, this was much better. Ben knew he'd enjoyed today far too much. Wanted Natalia—in so many ways—far too much. It made him reckless and weak, two characteristics he despised. Two characteristics he associated with his father... and his mother's heartbreak.

Yet even now he knew his self-control was slipping, notch by notch, until surely nothing would keep him from pulling her into his arms and losing himself in her as he was all too desperate to do.

Smiling grimly, he followed her out onto the dance floor where the writhing crowds would surely allow them both to keep their distance.

Natalia regretted taking Ben to the club as soon as they walked through the doors. The lights, the music, the noise—all of it was awful, and even though she'd been here a dozen times, she didn't want to be here with Ben. A place like this would only reinforce the unflattering assumptions he'd made about her. And really, Natalia thought as she turned to smile at him on the dance floor, she wanted to be alone with him, not hemmed in by a sweaty and indifferent crowd.

It surprised and even touched her that Ben had gone along with all of her plans today, that he was dancing even now, and she saw, he was actually a very good dancer. She would have expected a man like him—business-minded, focused and controlled—to move stiffly on the dance floor, or if she were honest, to sit on a bar stool and scroll through his emails on his BlackBerry.

But Ben moved with arrogant grace, his eyes glinting as if he knew exactly what she was thinking, Which he probably did. The man possessed an uncanny ability to read her mind. Know her heart.

Swallowing, Natalia looked away. Even amidst the safety of a crowd, she felt this magnetic pull, this insane craving to pull him closer, to lose herself in him. And if she did that... what would be left?

A few minutes after they started dancing the music suddenly changed to a low, lazy tune that had everyone pulling partners close. Natalia hesitated, half-wanting to run off the dance floor rather than face the fierce temptation of slow dancing with Ben. Or what if he walked off the floor first? He may have wanted to kiss her on a bet, but that didn't mean he wanted to dance with her. *Be* with her.

But already he was pulling her towards him, his hands firm on her hips, fingers splayed along her backside as he nestled her close against him. His lips brushed her hair as her arms twined round his neck almost of their own accord, so desperate was she for this contact. This closeness.

Natalia was barely aware of the music as she felt Ben's body against her own: his thigh against her hip, the evidence of his arousal pressing into her middle, his jaw almost touching her lips. Her body felt as if it were buzzing with awareness, pulsing with need. She pulled him closer, let her lips brush the stubble on his jaw, inhaled the clean, male scent of him as her senses swam and she heard—and felt—Ben shudder in response.

It felt so natural, so *obvious* to angle her head for the kiss they'd denied themselves all day. The kiss they surely both craved. Natalia's lips parted and Ben's mouth hovered above her own as she waited, aching, her whole body crying out for him to touch her.

'It could be a draw,' she whispered, her mouth so close to his they were almost—*almost*—kissing anyway. Her fingers curled round his shoulders as she swayed, not to the music, but from the desire flooding through her in a relentless river, sweeping her senses along with it. 'We both control the kiss,' she clarified huskily. She felt Ben's hands tighten on her hips, his fingers so strong and sure. 'We both win.'

She saw his lips curve in an answering smile, felt him pull her even closer, her breasts pressed against his chest, but he didn't bend his head. Didn't kiss her. Natalia flicked her gaze upwards, and although he was still smiling—a little—she saw the struggle in his eyes. The frustration, and maybe even the anger. Or was it despair?

Whatever stormy emotion battled in his eyes, it was one Natalia wished she hadn't seen. Wished Ben didn't feel.

He didn't *want* to kiss her.

Oh, he wanted her all right, wanted her perhaps as desperately as she wanted him. But he didn't want to want her, and that thought made sudden tears sting her eyes. With effort, despite the desire still coursing treacherously through her, she made herself pull away from him and walked off the dance floor.

Ben felt Natalia slip away from him and he cursed under his breath. He'd been so close to kissing her. So close to giving in, letting himself be swept away like he never had before. He knew, instinctively, elementally, that kissing Natalia would be like that. Kissing Natalia would change him, and he didn't want to be changed.

He should be relieved she'd broken it before he did, but he wasn't. He was annoyed and disappointed and incredibly sexually frustrated. Raking a hand through his hair, he followed her off the dance floor, searching the crowds for her familiar lithe frame.

He found her by the coat check, slipping on her snug little jacket. 'Is the fun over, then?' he asked lightly, and she didn't look at him as she answered.

'It most certainly is.'

Ben felt a flicker of guilty regret along with every other emotion twisting inside him and frying his brain. Why did this woman make him *feel* so much? He wasn't used to it. Didn't like it. Couldn't have it.

Yet he knew in that moment on the dance floor he'd hurt her somehow. Maybe she'd sensed his reluctance. Maybe— and this thought actually frightened him—she understood him better than he thought.

Neither of them spoke as Ben opened the passenger door for her, and then slid into the driver's seat. He thought about explaining, or apologizing, or *something*, but his thoughts were too tangled up inside him to separate, much less speak.

As the gate of the palazzo swung smoothly open and he drove up to the front of the magnificent building, he decided silence was better. Surely saying anything—explaining any-thing—would just drag them in deeper to this mess they'd found themselves in.

This mess of emotion and desire and need that Ben had never let himself feel before. The kind of mess his father made, and his mother endured. The kind of mess he never wanted for himself.

'Well.' Natalia cleared her throat, then shot him a cool smile. 'What can I say? It was fun.'

Ben nodded tersely. 'See you on the football pitch,' he said and for a second something flashed in her eyes, something Ben suspected was hurt, or perhaps sorrow. Her smile sud-denly seemed brittle.

'See you then,' she said, and slipped out of the car.

CHAPTER SEVEN

NATALIA blinked in the bright sunlight of Santina's football stadium and smoothed her hands down the sides of her baggy shorts. She felt ridiculously sloppy wearing what felt like a school PE kit, but Ben had been insistent that she dress appropriately for the first day of camp.

'And,' he'd told her, his mouth quirking upwards in that way she now recognised, 'that does not mean a miniskirt and stilettos.'

She would have felt better in a skirt, Natalia thought with a flicker of resentment. Safer and stronger. Fashion was one thing she *got*, one small way she felt successful.

'Ready to really work?' Ben asked, jogging up to her. He wore the same thing she did, and yet somehow it looked amazing on him. The T-shirt clung to the six-pack abs hiding under the thin fabric, and he wore his shorts slung low on his hips. Natalia could see his strong, muscular thighs and calves and she jerked her gaze upwards. She did not need any reminders of how his body had felt against hers; she'd been remembering all weekend. Yet clearly Ben was back to professional mode today, and if she hadn't experienced it herself, she wouldn't have believed he'd held her so close, he'd almost kissed her.

Almost.

'Are you saying I haven't been working already?' she enquired. 'Because I think a thousand envelopes would disagree.'

'Today you're going to really work. And get tired and muddy and sweaty.' Natalia wrinkled her nose, and Ben grinned, so obviously enjoying this. 'Come on, Princess. Let's get going. The kids are about to arrive.' And without any warning he tossed her a football. Natalia caught it out of instinct, but she heard the distinct sound of a nail breaking and with a little yelp she dropped the ball to inspect the damage.

'There goes your manicure,' Ben murmured as he walked by her. 'Can't say I didn't warn you.'

'Can't say you're a complete arse,' Natalia muttered back. 'Oh wait, I *can*.'

Ben just chuckled, his good humour clearly impossible to deflate. He was like a different man today, Natalia thought, alive and invigorated in a way she'd never seen him before. Except when he'd held her in his arms…he'd seemed pretty invigorated then. Yet Ben clearly wanted to forget that entire episode, and Natalia knew she should too. Unfortunately she couldn't stop thinking about it. Remembering. Wanting. Sighing, Natalia picked up the football and followed him to the front of the stadium. Dozens of children swarmed the gates, and several tables were set up for registration. Ben, she saw, was greeting each child with warm enthusiasm, an easy smile or a ruffle of their hair, his attitude laid-back and natural.

He glanced back at her, and then jerked his head towards one of the tables. 'Why don't you take names?'

'Take names?'

'Just write them down, Princess.' He turned back to the stream of kids coming through the gates, and Natalia made her way over to the makeshift table. Fabio was already there, taking children's names and writing them on a form. He pointed to a stack of name tags. 'Could you fill out those?'

'Certainly,' Natalia said after a moment. 'Of course.' She sat down next to Fabio and pulled a stack of name tags towards her and uncapped a pen. Then, smiling brightly, although her heart had started to thud with hard, painful beats, she looked up at the first child who came towards her, hesitant and shy. *'Como ti chiami?'*

'Paulo.'

'Ciao, Paulo.' Biting her lip hard in concentration, she started to write a *P*. And then an *A*. She had to think carefully about each stroke, knowing she was taking far too long, sensing the backup of kids restlessly waiting for their tags. Prickly heat burst all over her body and she knew she was going blotchy again. *Fabulous*. She bit down hard on her lip, willed that all-too-telling flush to fade. Finally she finished and passed the tag over to Paulo. He took it with murmured thanks, and Natalia saw it looked like it had been written by a child younger than he was.

The next child came forward. 'Gabriella.'

So many letters. Natalia started again. She could do this. She wasn't normally this slow, but the panic of performing in public, of knowing that any moment Ben might come over and demand why the princess was taking so long and couldn't she even *write* made her fingers tremble and the letters dance before her eyes.

She glanced up at Gabriella, a solemn-eyed little girl with a cloud of dark hair. 'You know what? I'm sure it would be faster if you did this.' She grabbed a handful of pens and started passing them out to each child, who gladly took them and began to write their own names on the tags.

Natalia slumped back in her chair in trembling relief. That had been a close one. Too close. She'd hid her disability for so long, first out of confusion and then from shame, and finally on command. She wasn't about to have it ripped out in the open now. Not by Ben. Not by anyone.

The kids had started to trickle away from the table, and she straightened, glancing over at Ben, who was organising the children into lines. She watched him covertly, noticing how confidently he strode across the pitch, how much he seemed to be enjoying this. She had never seen him look so relaxed or so…happy. She'd seen him look amused, or entertained, or interested, but he'd never actually seemed happy.

And neither had she.

'Natalia?' She started at the sound of her name. Ben was calling to her, and she stood, smoothing her T-shirt and shorts as if she could magically turn them into a silk blouse and tailored skirt. 'Would you help me show the kids how to dribble?'

Dribble? As if she had any idea what he was even talking about. She didn't even like *watching* football. 'Of course,' she said, giving him her gracious princess smile, and strode up to the pitch where Ben stood, the children all lined up neatly on one side. Ben explained to the children, in careful Italian which both surprised and touched her, how to dribble the ball, which, Natalia discovered, meant just kicking it with your feet. Then Ben punted the ball upwards off his foot and bounced it off his head, garnering a giggle from the crowd. He turned to Natalia, smiling, yet with the steel of challenge in his eyes. He could have chosen any of the other volunteers for this little exercise, but he'd chosen her. Of course. The children weren't the only ones Ben wanted to learn a lesson.

'Simple, right?'

'Oh, yes,' Natalia assured him. 'Simple.' Simpler, in any case, than writing name tags. She straightened, ready to show Ben just how well she could kick. Or dribble. Or whatever.

Ben dribbled the ball neatly between his feet and then sent a kick over to her. Natalia tensed, tried to kick it back, but the ball rolled right past her while her foot arced widely through the air, connecting with nothing. She heard a few snickers from the crowd of children, and felt her face burn.

She hated being laughed at. Hated, hated, *hated* it. It made her feel twelve years old again, her first year of boarding school, standing in front of her entire class while the teacher proclaimed in ringing tones, *Natalia Santina is the slowest girl in this school! She writes like a six-year-old!*

She still felt the shame. Slow. *Stupid.*

Taking a deep breath, she squared her shoulders and marched over to where the ball had come to a stop. Then she gave it a satisfyingly hard kick back towards Ben. He trapped it neatly between his feet, his eyebrows raised in question as he glanced her. As usual, he was able to guess something of her mood.

'Shall we try again?'

Natalia just shrugged. She felt unbearably tense and brittle, as if she might snap right in half. Ben kicked the ball again, slow this time, an obviously easy shot so she'd be able to kick it back.

She didn't.

Once again the ball rolled by her and her foot swung through the air. She heard a few children giggle from behind their hands.

Tears of frustration burned beneath her lids. Couldn't she do *anything* right? Ben was probably enjoying this, she thought savagely as she went to retrieve the ball. He'd probably been dreaming of this—Princess Natalia, humiliated on his football pitch! She grabbed the ball and threw it back to him, forgetting that in this wretched sport you weren't supposed to use your hands.

Ben caught the ball easily, giving her a quick, frowning look of concern before he turned back to the crowd of children. 'You get the idea?' he asked in his careful Italian. 'Why don't you pair up and practise dribbling and then kicking the ball back and forth.' He glanced back at her again, and Natalia knew he was wondering just what was going on. She folded her arms and did her best to look bored. She would not give him the satisfaction of knowing how that little episode had rattled her.

The children quickly paired up and Ben strolled between

them, offering pointers and encouragement. After a few moments he glanced back at her again and she could tell he wanted her to do something. But what? What could she do? She was so bloody *useless*. She'd never minded so much before.

Then she saw Ben's glance move to a little girl standing off to the side, one long dark strand of hair twirled around a finger. She was watching the kids all in pairs, happily dribbling and kicking away, and nobody noticed she was all alone. Natalia knew how that felt. She might be the party princess now, but she'd been the big loser in school.

Without even thinking about what she was doing, she jogged over to her and crouched down so she was eye-level. 'Gabriella, *sì*?' The girl nodded solemnly. 'You want to practice dribbling?' She shrugged, trying to act like she didn't care, but Natalia saw the eagerness in her eyes. She knew all about that too. Pretending you didn't care when you were dying inside. 'I don't have a partner,' Natalia said. 'Will you be my partner?' The girl shrugged again, clearly not wanting her pity. Another thing Natalia understood. 'Because,' she continued, 'you saw how terrible I was, didn't you? I can't even kick the ball, never mind this dribbling.' She was rewarded with a tiny smile. 'I think I'm the worst player on the pitch, so I hope you don't mind being my partner.'

A long moment passed where Gabriella just gazed at her with those sad, dark eyes. 'I don't mind,' she finally whispered, and she followed Natalia out onto the pitch. Natalia forced her own self-consciousness back as she attempted to dribble the ball between her feet before passing it to Gabriella. It really was harder than it looked. A lot harder. They managed a tentative back and forth for a few minutes and then Natalia went to give a big kick, missed the ball completely and fell flat on her back.

She lay there for a moment, the wind knocked right out of her, and blinked slowly up at the cloudless blue sky. Then she heard someone jogging towards her, and suddenly she was looking into Ben's face, close enough so she could see the sunlight glinting off the faint stubble on his chin. He gazed down at her, and Natalia saw a shadow of anxious concern in his eyes. He touched her cheek once, gently, before pulling his hand quickly away. He'd surprised them both by touching her. Staring up at him, Natalia suddenly felt breathless for an entirely different reason.

Ben sat back on his heels. 'You OK, Princess?'

She spread her arms and legs out as far as she could and managed a sunny smile. 'Never better.'

His mouth quirked upwards. 'That was quite a fall.'

'I know, it took me a long time to perfect it.' She moved, experimentally, wincing a little bit at how her back hurt. Ben frowned, placed a hand on her shoulder. Even in her bruised state she felt another jolt of awareness.

'Stay still. You might have hurt something.'

'I *know* I hurt something. But nothing's broken.' She eased herself up into a sitting position. 'Trust me, I'm a complete coward when it comes to pain.'

Ben was giving her a rather strange look. His hand remained on her shoulder. 'Somehow I doubt that.'

Discomfited, Natalia looked away from him and saw that the productivity on the pitch—all that dribbling and kicking—had come to a complete halt as a hundred pairs of eyes stared at her with a mixture of concern and amusement. Talk about humiliation.

Yet as Gabriella walked up to her, her eyes wide, Natalia found, to her own amazement, that she didn't really mind. Not this time. Not if it made just one child feel a little bit better about herself. She winked at Gabriella. 'I told you I was terrible, didn't I?' Gabriella gave a little laugh, and this time Natalia didn't feel like she was being laughed at. She had made the joke, not been the butt of it. She stood, trying not to wince because her back did really hurt, and held the ball out to Gabriella. 'Your turn, I think.'

'Maybe you should sit out—' Ben offered. He still looked rather touchingly concerned. Probably just his overblown sense of responsibility, Natalia told herself. It would be stupid to read anything more into it. To *want* more. She gave him a mocking look.

'Don't coddle the princess, hotshot. I can do it.'

A surprised smile quirked the corner of his mouth and his expression lightened. 'I know you can,' he said.

Ben watched Natalia walk away and felt a surprising surge of admiration—and maybe something else. Something deeper. The tangle of emotions he'd felt inside him since the day spent with Natalia had tuned into a knot that seemed to be taking over his body. His thoughts. His heart.

He'd spent far too much time thinking about that almost-kiss, as if it had meant something. As if it could have. In a desperate attempt at distraction he'd gone into the office on Sunday, hoping that piles of paperwork would keep him from remembering just how perfect Natalia had fit against him, how right she'd felt in his arms.

And it had worked, for a little while. Until he'd seen her again, and he'd been desperate to touch her, and then when she'd fallen he'd felt as if his world had spun on its axis and he'd run over to her, his heart pounding, his mouth dry with fear.

This woman made him feel too much. Want too much. And after witnessing his father's three marriages and his mother's ongoing heartbreak as she turned a determinedly blind eye to his philandering, Ben didn't want to feel or want anything, for any woman.

Do you believe in true love?

He *believed* in love, he just didn't like it. Or want it. His mother's love for his father certainly hadn't helped her any. He did not intend to fall into the same terrible trap.

And certainly not with Princess Natalia.

Ben watched the little girl kick the ball back to Natalia, and this time she actually stopped it with her foot— His thoughts came to a screeching halt. Why was he thinking about Natalia and love at all? She was a spoilt princess, shallow, vain, publicity-seeking. Everything he hated.

Except maybe she wasn't. He was starting to wonder if there really was something underneath that brittle la-di-da facade, to believe there was a real woman with a tender and vulnerable heart.

The thought both appalled and terrified him.

He wanted Natalia Santina to be exactly what he'd thought she was: shallow, selfish, spoilt and vain. It would be so much easier. He wouldn't have to wonder, or want, or find excuses to spend more time with her. He wouldn't be interested in her at all.

But he was, and knew he had been from the first moment she'd sauntered over to him at Allegra's engagement party. He'd sensed the spark between them then, and asking her to volunteer had been, he was afraid, just a way to spend time with her.

And the more time he spent with her, the more he wondered. The more he wanted. And he felt his precious control slipping notch by notch, until he'd lose it completely and nothing would keep him from taking her in his arms and demanding she tell him all her secrets. He wanted to *know* her…inside and out, and that thought scared him more than anything else.

By the end of the day Natalia's whole body ached. Ben was right. This *was* really working, and all she wanted was to fall into bed, tired, muddy and sweaty, just as Ben had promised she would be—and now was.

The children and most of the other volunteers had trooped out of the stadium at five o'clock, tired and happy, if as muddy as she was. Natalia hovered by the registration table, shuffling forms into piles and putting the pens back in the jar. She knew she should leave and yet she was strangely reluctant to. Despite the aches and pains, the dirt and mud, even the humiliation, she'd *enjoyed* today. She'd felt productive and useful, engaged and energised. Not that she'd ever let Ben Jackson know it. Still, the thought of returning to the palazzo with all of its expectations and strictures almost made her want to start kicking the ball around again. 'Not bad, Princess,' Ben said, and Natalia turned to see him coming back from the front of the stadium. She felt a frisson of awareness shiver up her spine as she took in his long-legged stride, his easy smile. Mud streaked his long, muscled legs and Natalia saw a splotch of it on his cheek.

'Not bad?' she repeated, arching an eyebrow. 'I've completely ruined my manicure and that's all you can say?'

He stopped in front of her, close enough that she could feel the heat coming from his body, inhale the tangy and not unpleasant scent of aftershave and male sweat.

'Let's see,' he said, and took one of her hands in his. Natalia tried to ignore the treacherous and tempting warmth that stole through her body at the feel of his roughened fingers touching her own. His thumb caressed her palm—surely he didn't even realise he was doing it—as he studied her now broken and chipped nails. He glanced up, and she saw the glints in his navy eyes, fixated on the quirk of that incredibly sensual and mobile mouth. 'A noble sacrifice,' he murmured. He didn't let go of her hand. Natalia heard her breath come out in something halfway to a shudder. Had Ben noticed? Did he realise what this simple hand-holding was *doing* to her?

She saw his pupils flare and dilate and with a thrill she realised he was as aware—and affected—as she was. The thought made her knees weaken in a way that had nothing to do with how exhausted and achey she was, and everything to do with the electric attraction that pulsed silently between them.

'I quite agree,' she said in a voice that bordered on shaky, and with both reluctance and determination tugged her hand from his own. This was way too dangerous.

Ben took a step back, raked a hand through his sweat-dampened hair. She really wasn't into all that macho male stuff—she'd always preferred men to be well-groomed and elegant—but right now she didn't think she'd seen anything half as sexy as Ben Jackson in his muddy football kit. 'Actually,' he said, 'you were amazing today.'

Natalia tried to ignore the rush of emotion his sincere praise caused to blaze through her. Emotion was just as dangerous as passion, maybe even more so. She didn't get close to anyone, not physically, not emotionally. She'd learned *those* lessons, at least. Yet right now Ben was breaching all of her defenses, leaving her completely exposed and wanting, and that knowledge made her go on the attack. 'That must have hurt,' she mocked, and he simply raised his eyebrows in query. 'Giving me a genuine compliment,' she clarified tartly.

'Actually, it didn't feel half bad.'

'High praise indeed then.'

He shook his head, smiling ruefully. 'You never let up, do you?'

No. Never. 'Would you really want me to?' she quipped, meaning it to be a throwaway remark, but she knew immediately that Ben had taken it all too seriously. From the shadow in his eyes, the way his lips thinned, she realised he was as wary of getting close as she was.

Why did that hurt?

Surely it should have only brought relief.

'I don't know about that, Princess,' he finally said, and Natalia knew from his lazy tone that he was playing this as she was. Light. Safe. 'I told you you were exhausting.'

'And I told you I move fast. Now I need to get back and shower up. I have a *very* important dinner engagement.'

She saw his expression harden and knew he was thinking about her reputation, the salacious reports of her behavior in the tabloids. That tell-all affair she'd supposedly had. Natalia smiled grimly. She'd agreed to the affair, just not the tell-all part. And *that* was surely another reason to steer clear of Ben Jackson. She didn't *do* close. She didn't let people in. She wasn't about to get her heart broken. Again.

'You'd better get going then,' he said, his tone turning cool as he swept one arm towards the gates of the stadium. 'Your driver must be waiting.'

No doubt he was envisioning just what she might she get up to tonight, and all she had was another boring dinner with foreign dignitaries intent on sizing her up like a side of meat.

'I'm sure he is,' she agreed, her tone as cool as his. Yet she didn't move. She had a crazy impulse to blurt something out to him, something she knew she would instantly regret. *You don't know me. I'm not like that. At least, I don't want to be.* She pressed her lips together, hardened her heart and walked past him.

'Have a nice night, Princess.' Ben's drawl seemed to follow her right out to the stadium's car park and the waiting car. And she still heard his mocking voice in her head all the way back to the palazzo.

CHAPTER EIGHT

'I HAVE a favour to ask of you.'

Natalia glanced up from the net bag of footballs she'd been collecting. It was the end of the third day of camp, and she felt as limp as a wet rag. She'd always worked out, but being on a football pitch for eight hours a day promised a whole new level of fitness.

'A favour?' she said, arching her eyebrows. It was the second week of camp, and she hadn't talked to Ben much outside of working hours. When she did she kept it light and mocking. Safe. 'I bet you don't like that.'

'Why wouldn't I?'

'I doubt you like asking favours of anyone.'

He frowned, considering this. It was one thing Natalia had learned and liked about him: he *thought* about things. Seriously. He wasn't dismissive. Except, perhaps, of her. 'I don't suppose I do,' he finally admitted.

'Especially of me.'

'Don't put yourself down, Princess.'

'Actually,' she said tartly, 'I was putting *you* down.' She drew the drawstring closed on the bag and tossed it with the others. The pitch was empty, the other volunteers having trickled away. She was conscious of the looming space all around them, the emptiness.

'Seriously,' Ben said. 'A favour.'

Natalia folded her arms. 'Okay. Tell me.'

'I have a client dinner on Friday,' Ben said. He sounded hesitant, which was a first. Natalia wasn't used to seeing him anything but arrogantly assured. 'They're interested in supporting these camps, making it more of a joint effort.'

'That's good, isn't it?'

Ben nodded. 'Their support would help to take the camps to the next level. Expand across Europe, maybe South America and Asia.'

'I always knew you were ambitious.'

'It would be great for the kids,' Ben said, and she saw a shadow of vulnerability in his eyes. This *meant* something to him, she realised. It meant a lot. 'All right,' she said quietly. 'What do you want me to do?'

'Come to the dinner with me. My clients want to meet you, and it would be great publicity for the camp.'

Natalia knew she could make any number of quips about how Ben really did want publicity after all, but suddenly she didn't feel like it. 'Want to meet me?' she echoed.

'They've heard of you.'

'Who hasn't?' she said drily, but she felt a little knife-twist of disappointment. She didn't want to play the princess to Ben's starstruck clients. She didn't want to play the princess at all. 'You realise,' she said after a moment, 'you might not get the kind of publicity you're looking for.'

'I'm aware of that,' Ben said evenly, and the knife twisted a little more. She knew he didn't mean to judge her, but he still was. At least, it felt like he was.

'Of course you are,' she agreed, and Ben's expression didn't flicker.

'I don't like the press,' he said quietly, a confession. 'I never have. I've seen the cost of it on too many people in my family. Especially my mother, after my father—well, I'm sure you know what my father did.' His mouth twisted, and Natalia knew how hard it was for him to admit this. Or anything.

'I don't know all he did, because I don't read the tabloids

as thoroughly as you clearly do,' she said, keeping her voice light. 'But I did hear that he wasn't exactly faithful.'

'Right.' He let out a slow, shuddering breath. 'And his philandering generated a great deal of press. That's why I jumped to conclusions when they snapped a photo of us coming out of the restaurant—I've lived with that kind of thing all my life.'

'So have I,' Natalia returned quietly, and Ben frowned.

'But you go after it. I've seen and know enough to realise that, Princess. You grant interviews, you pose for photographs, you attend all the parties and clubs where you know they'll see you and assume the worst.' He stared at her, hard, as if he was trying to strip away all her defenses and see right into her soul. 'Why do you do it if you don't like it?'

She said nothing, unwilling to be as honest as he'd been. She felt a pressure building in her chest and behind her eyes, and she was afraid what might happen if she gave in to it. If she said all the things she wanted to say. *Because it's the only way I know of being in control. Because I've been humiliated too many times and in too many ways and at least now it looks like I chose it. But I don't want you to think I'm really like that...even if I am.*

'Natalia?' Ben prompted, and she heard a thread of urgency in his voice. 'Tell me.'

And she wondered if he knew what he was asking, if he sensed the truth. She shook her head, shrugged. 'The press has its uses,' she managed, and turned to pick up the bag of footballs, anything to keep her from revealing too much. Ben's gaze alone was already far too knowing.

He didn't speak for a long moment. Finally, her back still turned, she heard him say, 'In any case this is just a quiet dinner at a discreet restaurant.'

'Fine.' Natalia turned back to him and forced a smile. She'd really enjoyed these past few days, getting dirty, playing with the kids, making Gabriella smile. Being real...and *not* being a princess. 'I suppose I could dust off my tiara. This Friday, you said?'

Ben nodded. 'I'll pick you up at five.'

Ben watched as Natalia walked away from him, her chin tilted at that haughty angle, her back ramrod straight. Her defensive position. He knew it well. He went over the exchange they'd just had, wondering how he'd hurt her, for she surely was hurt, even if she'd never admit it.

She was a woman of secrets, he knew, secrets she had no intention of telling him or anyone else. He could tell when she wasn't telling the truth, but he didn't know what the truth was. And he wanted to.

This was dangerous, Ben knew. He was drawing closer to her even though he'd told himself not to. Swaying with her on the dance floor had been enough of a test of his self-control, but this was more. Worse. Seeing her trying her best on the football pitch, getting dirty, making the kids smile, giving him one of her mocking looks...all of it made him seek her out more and more.

This dinner was really just a pretext to spend time with her outside of camp, he knew. At least he was honest with himself about that. His clients might have mentioned wanting to meet the princess, but he could have deflected them, or brought them to the camp one day when everyone was there. He wanted her to come out with him. He wanted her, full stop.

And he didn't know what to do about it. The wise and safe choice was to keep his distance, take her at face value, and let nothing shake his resolve or shatter his control.

Yet Ben didn't feel like being safe any more. Or wise. He'd always lived a life of admirable and consistent restraint, and he was *tired* of it. He wanted Natalia with a fierceness he'd never felt before, a fierceness that felt right even though it terrified him.

This he could not control.

* * *

At five o'clock on Friday Natalia stood in front of the ornate full-length mirror in her room and gazed at her reflection. She'd toyed with the idea of wearing something like her silver spangled dress, short and outrageous, and then decided against it. She was tired of titillation. It had been her cover for so long, her way of keeping people from getting too close and guessing all of her deficiencies, but she didn't want to do it tonight. She wasn't sure she wanted to ever again.

And where, Natalia wondered, did that leave her? Who then could she *be*? She didn't really have an answer. Sighing, she reached for a stunning diamond and emerald necklace that was part of her mother's crown jewels. Made of twenty-four emeralds, each one surrounded by diamonds, the largest one at the center, nestling between her breasts, it was a magnificent piece of jewelry. Natalia had always thought it a bit ostentatious, not to mention heavy to wear, but she felt, for the sake of Ben's clients, she'd better look every inch the princess tonight.

She paired the necklace with a starkly elegant cocktail dress in black silk that skimmed her curves and then flared out around her knees. The dress was elegant yet simple, making it a perfect backdrop for the necklace. She picked a pair of skyscraper heels with diamante straps to make the outfit a little less severe. A girl still had to have a *little* fun.

A knock sounded on her bedroom door, and her personal maid peeked in. 'Mr Jackson is downstairs, Your Highness.'

'Thank you, Ana.' Natalia gave her reflection one more glance and, satisfied, reached for the silk fringed shawl and beaded clutch that matched her dress and headed downstairs.

Her breath dried in her throat at the sight of Ben in the palazzo's soaring entrance hall. He wore a suit, just as he had at the engagement party and every day at the office, so there was no reason for him to look any different than before. Or for her to *feel* any different, and yet she did. Maybe it was the shared history they had now, or perhaps just this attraction she could no longer pretend to deny. Her gaze was help-lessly drawn to his long, lithe body, the suit expertly tailored to showcase muscular legs, trim hips and powerful shoulders. The crisp white shirt and cobalt-blue silk tie emphasised the lean planes of his jaw and cheek, the steely blue of his eyes. He looked elegant and powerful, and it was an intoxicating combination.

Her legs felt a little trembly as she came down the marble staircase, Ben's gaze intent upon her. He stretched out one hand towards her as she came to the last stair.

'Good evening, Princess.' For the first time her title didn't feel like a mockery or sneer. It felt almost like an endearment. She smiled and took his hand.

'Good evening.'

He nodded a farewell towards the liveried attendants standing sentry in the hall, and then led her out into the night. She felt a little bit like Cinderella, leaving the castle instead of going to it. And that was how she wanted it. As she breathed in the sultry night air she felt free. Free and maybe even happy, or at least something close to it.

'So where are we going at such an unfashionably early hour?' she asked as Ben opened the passenger door of his silver luxury model car.

'Our dinner reservation is actually at eight. It's going to take a little while to get there.'

'A little while? You can drive the length of Santina in under two hours.'

Ben's smile gleamed in the darkness as he started the car and drove smoothly down the palazzo's curving drive and through the gates. 'I never said we were going somewhere on Santina.'

His meaning was made clear when he pulled up to the island's only airport fifteen minutes later. Natalia skidded to a halt in her stilettos as she stared at the tiny plane Ben had led her to in one remote corner of the airfield.

'We're going in *that*?'

'My private jet,' Ben said with just a touch of irony.

'Let me tell you something, hotshot. For me, private jet means champagne, caviar and leather sofas. Not—' She took a step forward so she could better inspect the plane. 'A piece of cardboard and some chewing gum.'

'I'll have you know this is a Seabird Seeker 360, and it's an amazing piece of equipment. It also cost four hundred thousand dollars.'

She folded her arms. 'I'm sorry to say you got a *very* bad deal.'

'Princess,' Ben said with a thread of laughter in his voice, 'are you *scared*?'

Natalia drew herself up and eyed the plane warily. 'As a matter of fact,' she told him, 'yes. And not ashamed to admit it.' For once.

Ben reached for one hand and lazily pulled her towards him. Natalia came reluctantly, more afraid to get so close to him than going up in that flimsy excuse for an airplane. 'Come on, Natalia,' he said softly. 'I'll keep you safe.'

And Natalia wondered if he was talking about flying in the Seabird, or something else entirely. Something far more important and frightening. Her heart thudded against her ribs and she managed a light laugh only with effort.

'Let me see your pilot's license.'

'You don't trust me?' He was still holding her hand, the other hand resting lightly on her back, and he'd drawn her so close the hem of her dress brushed against his legs. She breathed in the now-familiar scent of his aftershave and felt, quite literally, dizzy.

'Not an inch,' she managed, and made herself draw back.

Ben let her go. 'If you're really scared, we can charter a bigger plane,' he said, his tone turning serious. 'I made sure there was one available.'

His thoughtfulness touched her, even though she didn't

want it to. She didn't want this man to affect her, to slip under her defenses so easily, and yet right now, in the sultry darkness with him standing so close, she couldn't quite summon one of her cutting remarks that had served her so well in the past. 'Let me at least take a look at this thing,' she said, and turned towards the plane.

It was *very* cozy. Two leather seats side by side in a cockpit, and glass all around. Flying in it would, Natalia thought, be amazing. If she let herself go. If she trusted Ben.

Why was *that* thought so scary, far more frightening than actually getting inside this piece of scrap metal?

'Well?' Ben asked. She'd clambered up so she was halfway into the cockpit, and she could sense Ben's presence behind her, feel the heat of him.

'I suppose it might be all right,' she said grudgingly, and Ben let out a dry chuckle.

'High praise from the princess. Get in.' He put his hands on her hips and guided her into the low-slung seat, sending a flare of awareness and heat low through her pelvis. Yes, she thought, swallowing drily, this really was quite cozy.

Ben felt a jagged jolt of desire ricochet from his hands through his whole body. He couldn't keep from touching her. He watched Natalia settle into her seat, and he could still feel the curve of her hips on his palms, imagine pulling her closer, fitting her to him.

He forced the thought away and slid into his own seat. 'You sure you can fly this thing?' she asked, and he slid her a knowing smile.

'Watch me.'

'Oh, I will.'

Was he imagining the wicked innuendo in her voice? He knew he felt it. Everything about this whole evening felt agonisingly charged, even more than the last time they'd been out together. For even with the ultimate distraction of Natalia sitting less than a foot away from him, her skin so smooth and golden, the dress hugging the curve of her breasts and the dip of her waist so lovingly, he realised something else. Something deeper.

He was *happy*.

When had he last felt this relaxed with a woman? When had he last enjoying just *being* with someone so much? He couldn't remember. Maybe never. And even though the more rational part of his mind was insisting that this was *Natalia*, spoilt party princess whose exploits featured in nearly every tabloid, the rest of him wanted to drown out that nagging whine and just relax. Enjoy.

Be happy.

He started taxiing down the runway. Natalia gripped the leather armrest. 'You're not actually phobic, are you?' he asked in genuine concern, and she gave him another one of her wicked looks.

'A little late to ask me that, isn't it?'

He let out a dry laugh. 'I suppose so.'

'Fortunately I'm not. I'm scared of plenty of things, but not flying. Although I've never flown in a tin can before, so I suppose I could nurture a bit of phobia if I put my mind to it.'

'What are you afraid of then?' Ben asked, genuinely curious.

Natalia shrugged. 'The usual things. The dark, for one.'

'The *dark*?'

She gave him an annoyed look. 'I didn't say I was completely phobic about it. I just don't like being alone in a dark room.'

'Do you have a night light?' He spoke at least half teasingly, but she answered in seriousness.

'I keep the bathroom light on.'

'You're not scared of the dark out there, are you?' he said, nodding to the expanse of sky that was just starting to darken to violet.

Natalia let out a little hiss of breath. 'No, of course not. I mean, the *dark*. Like a cupboard with no light at all.'

A cupboard? It sounded like she'd had some kind of bad experience. Ben decided not to press. He hadn't meant to tease her; he just couldn't imagine Natalia being afraid of anything. She seemed so fearless. 'What else?' he asked. The Seabird was gaining speed and Natalia didn't answer as they took off into that endless stretch of sky, the horizon a vivid streak of magenta as the sun slid below the sea.

'No, now it's your turn,' she said when the Seabird levelled out. 'What are you afraid of?'

Ben flexed his hands on the controls and considered. 'Something bad happening to someone in my family,' he said at last.

Natalia rolled her eyes. 'I could have told you that. You are a complete control freak. I'm sure you feel responsible for everyone in your family, even your parents.'

'And that's a bad thing?' Ben asked drily, although in truth he felt a bit disconcerted by her perception.

'I don't know, I haven't asked your family.' She wiggled a little bit in her seat, getting comfortable, and Ben was momentarily distracted by the sight of her dress sliding around, that huge emerald swinging in the shadowy V between her breasts. 'Anyway,' she resumed, clearly more comfortable now, although Ben was decidedly *not*, 'I mean, what are you really afraid of? Your deepest, darkest, most secret fear.'

He gave her an amused look, although he was definitely feeling uncomfortable in a whole variety of ways. 'And why should I tell you that?'

She slid him a slyly challenging look from under her lashes. 'Scared?'

'No. I'm just not sure I want the next headline of the local rag to be *Ben Jackson: The Truth About His Phobia of Spiders*.'

She let out a little laugh, but it sounded brittle. He'd been teasing—sort of—but he had the feeling he'd hurt her with his deflective remark, bringing in the stupid press. Again. And all he'd been trying to do was take the glare of her scrutiny away from himself.

'I don't actually talk to the press that much,' she said, staring out at the darkening sky. 'Despite what you think. They make most of it up all on their own.'

'I know they do.' He didn't really want to talk about her press coverage.

'It's just easier,' she continued, a surprising tremble in her voice, 'to try to control it. Or at least feel like you do. You know?' She turned to face him, and he saw a new vulnerability shining in her eyes, making them glitter like sunlight off a puddle.

He stared at her, sifting her words, looking for truth. 'Are you saying you seek that kind of publicity because it makes you feel better?' he asked, and heard the blatant disbelief in his voice. As someone who had avoided that kind of attention forever, it seemed like an incredibly foolish thing to do.

She stared back at him, her eyes shadowed. Guarded. 'That and I can't get enough of seeing myself in the papers,' she said lightly, and Ben knew she wasn't telling the truth. She was hiding behind another cutting, self-deprecating remark because that was what she did. Everyone had their defense mechanisms, their ways to stay safe. Natalia's just happened to be very different than his.

Her expression lightened and she gave him a challenging smile, all traces of vulnerability gone. 'You know what I think you're scared of?'

He eyed her in wary bemusement. 'What?'

'Of being scared.'

'The only thing we have to fear is fear itself?' he quoted drily.

'Roosevelt said it better, I suppose, but it's still true. You're afraid of feeling weak and out of control and helpless.'

Ben's hand tightened on the controls. He felt as if she'd just flayed him alive with her words, her perception. 'I didn't know you were such a history buff,' he finally said, and she laughed softly.

'I'm not the only one who likes to deflect personal questions, I see.'

'Well, that was really *quite* personal.'

'And true.'

'So why are you scared of the dark?' he asked, and felt Natalia tense. Amazed at how attuned he was to her moods and her body. He glanced at her, saw the strap of her dress had fallen a little down one golden shoulder. Yes, definitely her body.

'Does there have to be a reason?'

'There usually is.'

'Why are you scared of being scared?' she shot back, and suddenly Ben burst out laughing.

'Oh, Princess,' he said, 'maybe we should change the subject. Two guarded people asking each other invasive questions is surely a recipe for disaster.'

'Or at least a few awkward pauses,' Natalia agreed with a little laugh of her own. 'Fine. How long have you had your pilot's license?'

'I never actually said I had my pilot's license.'

She widened her eyes in mock horror. 'You *lied* to me?'

'Five years.'

'Why do you like flying?'

'This is starting to get personal, Princess.'

'Really? *That's* personal? You are quite the closed book.'

'So are you.' He slid her a thoughtful look. 'A lot more closed than I thought.' With more secrets and depths than he'd realised. Or even wanted.

She turned away from him and he could see the curve of her cheek, the angle of her jaw. In profile she seemed softer somehow. Vulnerable. He felt that protective tug again and resented it. They should stop this conversation. He didn't actually want to get close with someone like Natalia.

Did he?

Yet as the darkness of the sky and sea stretched out in front of them, Ben realised he didn't know what he wanted any more.

Natalia stared out at the darkness dropping like a velvet curtain all around them. Far below she could see a few twinkling lights, perhaps from a pleasure yacht cruising on the Mediterranean. She felt bizarrely unsettled and excited at the same time. Talking to Ben had energised her in a way nothing else had or could. Scared her too. She wasn't used to telling anybody…well, anything. At least, anything important.

And yet in the space of a few minutes she'd told Ben secrets no one else knew, like her fear of the dark. Why she courted the press. What was it about this man, Natalia wondered, that made her want to spill her secrets? Be *known*?

'You didn't actually tell me where we're going,' she said, determined to keep the conversation light. Impersonal. Surely that was what Ben wanted too.

'Rome.'

'Very nice. What restaurant?'

'Il Pagliaccio, on via dei Banchi.'

Natalia nodded. She knew it to be sophisticated, elegant and discreet. She leaned forward to gaze out at the sweep of sea below them, now barely visible in the darkness of night. 'So you keep a plane on the island? Is that how you get back and forth from London?'

'Generally.'

'How long are you going to stay on Santina? It must be difficult to be away from work for so long.'

'I telecommute, but no, it's not ideal. I'll stay till the end of the camp, wrap a few things up and then head back to London.'

So a couple of more weeks at most. Natalia felt an icy plunging sensation in her stomach, and realised it was disappointment. How ridiculous. She didn't even like Ben Jackson…except she couldn't really say that any more, could she? She was certainly attracted to him. And she was afraid she might feel even more than that. There was something so *steady* about Ben, so strong and true. She trusted him…perhaps even with her secrets.

She glanced over at him, his gaze steady on the sky, his hands relaxed on the controls. She let her gaze wander over the strong line of his jaw, the powerful curve of his shoulder, the crisp whiteness of his shirt emphasising the tanned column of his throat. He was a beautiful man, she thought with a throb of desire. She wanted to run her fingers along his jaw, loosen that tie and undo the buttons of his shirt, spread her hands along the taut, warm skin of his bare chest….

With a gulp Natalia turned away to stare blindly out the window. How was she going to get through this evening without touching him?

'Just a few more minutes,' Ben said, jerking her from her dazed thoughts, and she managed a smile and a stiff nod.

'Wonderful.'

A chauffeured limousine was waiting for them at the airport. Ben placed a hand low on Natalia's back as he guided her into the car. She could feel the heat of his fingers through the thin fabric of her dress, felt her body's basic and instinctive response to that gentle pressure. This was, she thought with a flutter of panic, going to be a very long evening.

A different kind of anxiety assailed her as they entered the elegant interior of Il Pagliaccio. What did these clients of Ben's know about her? What had they read—and what had they believed? She swallowed drily, suddenly feeling sick. She didn't want to be the party princess any more. She wanted to be someone else—someone she'd never dared let herself be.

Herself.

Yet did she really even know who that was any more? 'Natalia?' Ben touched her shoulder, his eyes shadowed with concern. 'Are you all right?'

'Yes, of course.' She forced herself to give him one of her usual flirty smiles. 'Why wouldn't I be?'

'Because you're looking like you're about to face your own execution,' Ben said drily. 'I thought this kind of thing was right up your alley.'

Of course he did. And it *was*. Hadn't she made sure it was? Hadn't she made that choice years ago, when she realised she could be enslaved to the press and their vicious mockery or embrace it? She'd had a choice. She'd made it. Surely it was far too late for regrets. It was far too late to want to be someone else—or want someone to believe you were someone else. Someone real.

'I'm fine,' Natalia said firmly, and with a coolly challenging smile she swept past Ben into the dining room. She hadn't been sure what to expect of Ben's clients, but they were all charming, urbane men who treated Natalia with both deference and respect. She saw one or two eye her speculatively on occasion, obviously wondering just how much of what they'd read was true. Natalia didn't give them a chance to find out. She listened when they spoke, laughed when they told jokes and behaved with gracious aplomb throughout the entire evening. She played the princess, and it was exhausting.

Life had always been a performance; she understood and accepted that. Act like you know the answer. Act like you don't care. Act like you think someone is interesting or attractive or funny. Act. Act. *Act*.

What happened when she didn't want to act any more? When the curtain came down, and the mask came off? What happened, Natalia thought even as she smiled and listened and laughed, when she stopped acting?

She didn't have an answer, and the not knowing exhausted her as much as anything else. Scared her too. As their main

courses were cleared, she excused herself from the table and
went to find a few minutes' solitude in the ladies'.

The room was blessedly empty and Natalia powdered her
nose and refreshed her lipstick, touching up her hair and
makeup with easy expertise. She was adding some mascara
to her eyelash when she caught an unguarded glimpse of herself in the mirror from the corner of her eye, and she felt as if
she'd just seen a stranger, someone she'd never met. Herself.

Slowly she lowered the mascara wand and stared at her
own face. On the surface it was, of course, completely recog-
nisable. She looked good. Pretty, maybe even beautiful. Her
eyes glinted and her mouth curved in her trademark, mocking smile. Princess Natalia. The Party Princess. Then she
blinked, and her smile disappeared, and she was left with a
face she didn't know. A face with wide, sad eyes and a mouth
that trembled with uncertainty. The face of the person she
really was…whomever that woman turned out to be.

Did anyone really want to find out? Did she? Did *Ben*?

Two women, chatting loudly in Italian, came into the room
and quickly Natalia capped her mascara, gave them a fleeting smile and hurried out.

In the narrow corridor that led back to the main restaurant
a man was leaning against the wall. Natalia assumed he was
talking on his mobile, and she murmured her excuse as she
brushed past him. He grabbed her elbow.

She stiffened, turned and recognised one of the men from
this evening. Brian, the one who had eyed her so speculatively. She felt a twist of disappointment; this evening wasn't
going to be any different. *She* wasn't different. She couldn't
be.

'Your Highness…'

She gave him a freezing stare. 'Excuse me,' she said with
haughty politeness, 'but I believe you are holding my elbow.'

He looked both startled and apologetic and to Natalia's
relief he let go, but he didn't move and she couldn't get by

without squeezing past him. She stared him down as coldly
as she could.

'I just wondered, Your Highness…' he slurred, clearly
more than a little drunk. 'I heard you like sailing and I have
a sweet little yacht you might like to see…if you know what
I mean.'

'Don't believe everything you read in the papers, Brian,'
Natalia said coolly. She knew he was referring to a ridiculous
article about a three-day orgy she'd supposedly indulged in
on a yacht last summer. The reality had been far tamer, and
frankly rather boring.

'I just thought…' he mumbled, starting to blush. Natalia
almost took pity on him.

'Don't embarrass yourself any further,' she advised, and
started to move past him. Her hip nudged his and yet something else caused a bolt of awareness to electrify her like
lightning, rooting her to the spot, freezing her senses. She
looked up and saw Ben blocking the entrance to the corridor, his expression completely and dangerously unreadable.

CHAPTER NINE

BEN wasn't prepared for the blaze of jealousy that fired through him at the sight of Natalia standing so close to his client, their heads bent together, their lips mere inches apart. Clearly they were having a cozy tête-à-tête, he thought savagely. Perhaps they were planning to meet up later for a drink—or more. A lot more. Natalia would give Ben one of her sly smiles and slip away from him, as insubstantial as smoke, as trustworthy as a broken promise. And then she'd leave with Brian. The thoughts raced through his mind, exploded like fireworks, obliterating all rational thought.

Then Natalia looked up and he saw her eyes widen, her body freeze, as tense as a bowstring, and his doubts disappeared in an instant. He was being ridiculous. He knew this woman too well. He *knew* her. And she wasn't flirting. Not with Brian anyway.

Yet the realisation that came on the heels of the first was far more alarming, far more frightening. Why the hell was he so jealous? Why did he care what Natalia did—or with whom? And how could he really know someone like Natalia, even if he wanted to?

'Ben…' she said, her voice little more than a whisper.

'Brian,' Ben said coolly, inclining his head in acknowledgement. He knew what Brian had been doing, loitering by the ladies' room. He bet Natalia did too.

Brian hurried past with some mumbled apology, and Ben

was left alone with Natalia. His heart was pounding, adrenalin racing through him from both the assumptions and unwelcome discoveries he'd made. They stared at each other,
unmoving, transfixed, and the moment stretched into something taut and focused, as if they were balanced on a pinpoint, a knife's edge.

'I wasn't—' she began.

'I know,' Ben said, closing the space between them in a
few long strides. Then he did what he'd been aching to do
for far too long.

He kissed her.

It wasn't gentle. It wasn't sweet or thoughtful; he didn't
ask permission. He kissed her with all the raw pent-up fury
he'd felt and had been feeling for far too long for wanting
this woman at all.

And she kissed him back the same way.

This woman gave as good as she got, Ben thought, *always*. And then he stopped thinking because his mind was
on overdrive registering the softness of Natalia's mouth, the
feel of her body pressed against his, his thigh already moving insistently between her legs, the citrusy scent of her perfume and the ragged gasp of her breath that drove him *mad*.

Their mouths still locked, he half stumbled with her until
her back came against the wall, and his hands were already
under her skirt, skimming the silky skin of her thighs. He'd
never been so driven by need. Talk about being out of control and weak and helpless. This was desire; this was fear.

She arched towards him, her head dropping back, one leg
twining around his, pulling him closer, her nails digging into
his back. Her breath came in short mewing gasps as he took
mastery of her mouth, his tongue delving into and discover-
ing the depths of her softness.

Then a door opened, and he heard a burst of feminine
laughter. Disoriented, he lifted his head from Natalia's and
saw two women standing in the doorway of the ladies' room.

He registered their amused expressions and Natalia's dazed one, but before he could step back or do anything at all she'd already slipped past him and was disappearing down the hallway, her heels clicking on the tile floor, her hands smoothing her rumpled skirt. Then she was gone.

Natalia forced herself not to tremble as she walked down that endless corridor. Her legs felt so wobbly she was amazed she could even stand. She pressed one shaking hand to her mouth. Her lips felt tender, swollen. She'd *never* been kissed like that before. When she'd met Ben she'd noticed his latent strength, leashed fury. She'd wondered what would happen if he lost control. Well, now she had an inkling and it scared her half to death.

She wasn't ready for that much passion. That much emotion. That much everything. A man like Ben…he'd demand everything from her. He'd take it too. *And then what would be left?* She'd thought she wanted to be known; she'd wanted someone to understand her. But now the thought filled her with a panicky fear.

'Princess Natalia!' The men chivalrously stood as she came back to the table. Smiling graciously, utterly refusing to think about what had just happened, Natalia sat down and proceeded to play the princess like she never had before.

Two hours later she and Ben were back at the airport. Natalia felt as brittle as a bone, as if she might snap or break at any moment. They hadn't spoken since they'd left the restaurant, and the very air was taut with unspoken questions. She wanted to say something just to break it, but her mouth was too dry to form a word.

She'd *never* felt like this before.

'After you,' Ben murmured as she slipped out of the limo, and with a huge effort Natalia finally managed to regain some of her insouciant composure.

'I think that went rather well, don't you?'

'A roaring success,' Ben agreed without expression. Natalia didn't look at him as she clambered up into the airplane. Good Lord, it was small. It had seemed cozy when they'd flown to Rome; now it felt positively airless. She couldn't breathe. She stared out the other window as Ben climbed into the cockpit and adjusted the controls.

He didn't speak again as the little plane took off into the night sky. Soon Rome was nothing but a cluster of tiny pin-pricks of light beneath them. Natalia leaned her head back against the seat and let out a shuddering sigh. Ben gave her a sideways glance.

'Tired?'

'Exhausted,' she admitted.

'So does acting the princess wear you out?'

'Completely.' And that kiss—and all it might mean—had drained her too.

'I would have thought it would revitalise you,' Ben said, a slight edge to his voice. 'Don't extroverts get their energy from socialising?' He spoke with a trace of mockery that was all too familiar. So it was going to be like that. *Fine.* That was what she wanted, wasn't it? Light. Safe. Not *real.* Not like that kiss had been.

'Perhaps I'm not an extrovert,' she said, her head still resting against the seat, her eyes closed. Ben let out a short little laugh.

'Not an extrovert, Princess? I find that hard to believe.'

She opened her eyes, turning her head so she could look at him. His shoulders were tense, a muscle bunched in his jaw. 'You don't know me,' she said quietly. 'Even if you think you do.' Even if she wanted him to. Even if she was afraid for him to.

Ben was silent as he gazed back out at the night, his hands flexing on the plane's controls. 'What are you saying?' he finally asked. 'That you don't enjoy all those parties? All those affairs and scandals? Everything you get up to—it's just an act?'

That's exactly what I'm saying. The words were in her heart, on her lips, yet she could not speak them. She'd tried telling him earlier, tried to explain she did it as a way to feel in control. *Strong.* But she knew now she could not risk making herself so vulnerable, not when it was so obviously *not* what Ben wanted to hear. He wanted her to be exactly what he thought she was. The shallow, spoilt princess. That was easier for both of them, wasn't it? Anything else was scary. And this was a man who hated fear, who was scared of being scared. He might not know her, but she understood him all too well.

She turned her head away from him and closed her eyes. 'An act?' she repeated with a little laugh. 'How exhausting it sounds.' Ben didn't reply, and neither of them spoke again.

By the time the plane landed on the airfield with a bump Natalia felt more depressed than tense. The hour of silence had left her with far too much time to think. To remember. She could quite distinctly and deliciously remember the feel of Ben's lips on hers, his hands sliding under her dress, those strong arms pulling her closer. It had all felt so amazing, and not just physically. Emotionally she'd felt something too. She'd felt something stir to life and awaken inside her that was more than just desire or need. Natalia was afraid to think of what it was.

She could not fall in love with this man.

She'd slid him a couple of sideways glances during the course of the journey, but his rather grim gaze remained on the stretch of night sky in front of them. She had no idea what he was thinking. Was he regretting the kiss? Wishing it had never happened? Why *had* he kissed her? Was it just simple lust or something more?

And was she willing to ask herself the same question? What was this potent mix of excitement and fear, hope and need, that she was feeling? If she ignored it, would it go away? Would life be safe again? Did she want it to be?

Too many questions, and no answers. She felt as if she were teetering on the edge of a precipice. She had no idea what lay waiting for her far below, or on the other side. She had no idea just how far she'd have to jump to land safely. Maybe she didn't even want to be safe any more.

'We're here,' Ben said, startling Natalia out of the endless looping reel of her thoughts. She straightened, smoothed her skirt.

'Brilliant,' she said, and cleared her throat, the sound loud and awkward in the confined space of the cockpit. Ben turned to look at her, and Natalia's breath froze in her chest.

'About that kiss…' he began.

Here it comes, she thought. The apologies or accusations, it didn't matter which. *It was a mistake. Let's forget it ever happened.* Maybe that would be for the best. Safer. She lifted her chin a notch. 'What about it?'

Ben stared at her for a long, endless moment. It was too dark for Natalia to make out his expression. 'I can't stop thinking about it,' he finally confessed in a ragged whisper, and then he was pulling her towards him, and she was on his lap and his mouth was on hers and that was all they needed to say about that kiss.

This one was even better.

Ben's hands slid along her body, his thumbs grazing the sides of her breasts before coming to rest on her hips, guiding her even closer so her legs splayed on either side of him, her body pressed intimately to his. It felt so good, Natalia thought hazily, but not good enough. She wanted more. She *needed* more. She shifted, pressing against him, her fingers fisted in his hair, raked his back in an agony of sensation, anything to get closer.

His hands were hard on her hips as he pressed back, and desperately Natalia thought how they were wearing too many clothes. Too much between them. Ben must have thought so too for impatiently his hands pulled at her dress, her underwear, his fingers finding her, and Natalia lost all train of thought, the sensation was too great, too *much*.

Until the cockpit was suddenly awash with light and someone tapped on the hatch of the plane. Ben jerked his mouth from hers and in one quick movement pushed her from his lap so she was sprawled most inelegantly, her dress up around her waist, half on her seat, half on the floor.

Natalia blinked, too shocked to even push her dress back down. One of the airport's security guards was shining a torch into the plane, but he'd immediately grasped what was going on for he backed quickly away.

'*Scusi...scusi...*'

Reality returned in a sickening rush. Humiliation too. Carefully Natalia pulled her dress back down.

'Sorry,' Ben muttered, and reached for her hand. Natalia ignored it. It wasn't easy to act sophisticated when she'd just been dumped on the floor, but she tried.

'That's not quite how I envisioned this ending,' she murmured, giving him a tart look even though inside she felt sick with humiliation and hurt.

'I thought it was the press.'

Ah. Well, that explained it. The last thing Ben wanted was to be caught *in flagrante* with Princess Natalia. 'The press, camping out at the airport after midnight?' she remarked drily. 'I know you don't like the paparazzi, Ben, but I think that's verging on paranoid.'

'Sorry,' he said again. He didn't look at her as he said it. Natalia felt her heart start to splinter.

'Sorry you thought it was the press, or sorry for dumping me on the floor like so much rubbish? Or,' Natalia continued, making sure to keep her voice dry, as if this were all so *amusing*, 'sorry for kissing me in the first place?'

Ben didn't answer. His expression had become so irritatingly unreadable. 'Perhaps you're sorry for all three?' she suggested. 'That would be a nice hat trick.' Ben remained silent and she finished adjusting her dress, her chin held high, her hands trembling.

'I'll drive you home,' he said after another interminable moment, and Natalia didn't bother to reply. She didn't think she could.

Nothing had gone the way he'd expected. Fury and regret pulsed through him as Ben drove Natalia home. She sat next to him, her posture ramrod straight, her chin tilted at an impossibly proud angle. Had he hurt her?

Of course you did, you bastard.

He'd dumped her on the floor. He'd pushed her away from him as if she disgusted him. It had been an instinctive response, one borne of self-protection and even fear. He'd had his moments of weakness exploited all too often. A tear-streaked face at four years old. Sullen and alone at twelve. The agony of his knee injury at sixteen. The paparazzi had captured every moment of emotional vulnerability and anguish he'd ever experienced and plastered them across their papers so the whole world had seen. So his mother had seen, and been heartbroken. *Oldest Jackson misses his Daddy. Another Jackson Disappoints. Ben Jackson's Dreams Shattered.*

He'd lived through it all, and he would not do so again. He'd spent his life, his whole damn life, trying to live a quiet life, worthy of respect and out of the glare of the media. Trying to give the Jackson name the respect it had once earned. He'd thought he could have done it with football, but when that failed—when *he* failed—he did it with business. All along he'd wanted to make a difference, to change the way people thought about his family, and in one sordid moment he could have ruined it all. That's what had gone through his head in a lightning-flash of fear when the cockpit had suddenly blazed with light. And while his history might have justified the fear, it certainly didn't excuse the way he'd just treated Natalia.

He'd been foolish, he supposed, to have taken her out at all, and yet even so he couldn't regret it. He'd wanted to be with her…and he still did.

Even now he wanted her, and not just physically, although that was certainly foremost in his mind. He wanted to apologise, explain why he was so afraid, and not just of the press, Ben realised in a rush of painful self-recrimination. Maybe that was just an easy excuse. He was afraid of himself. Afraid of losing control, of letting himself go because heaven only knew when Natalia was in his arms his whole world spun on its axis. Natalia had been right; he didn't like feeling weak and helpless and out of control. He *hated* it.

You're afraid of being afraid.

He pulled up to the palazzo and put on the emergency brake, turning to look at Natalia, to *say* something, but she'd already opened the door, her face angled away from him. 'Natalia…'

She turned to him with one of her old mocking smiles, but he could tell her heart wasn't in it. His wasn't either. 'Thank you for an evening that was *full* of surprises,' she said, and without waiting for a reply, she waggled her fingers in farewell and then disappeared into the palazzo.

Ben cursed aloud.

Thank goodness it was the weekend. She didn't have to see Ben for two whole days. Maybe, Natalia hoped, knowing it was futile, she'd have put the whole sorry episode behind her by Monday morning. Maybe she'd have forgotten it completely, or at least stopped remembering the sweet slide of his lips against hers every second of the day.

The weekend was endless. She thought about him constantly, wondered what he was thinking. Feeling. Wearing, even. She felt like a teenager with a first crush, except she'd never felt like this as a teen. This was deeper, darker, more dangerous, and yet infinitely sweeter too, and that made it all the more painful.

She relived the moment he'd pushed her away from him over and over again. He'd acted out of instinct, which made it worse. He'd been desperate to distance himself and the thought hurt more than it should. It shouldn't hurt at all; it had just been a kiss.

A lot more than a kiss, Natalia acknowledged grimly. A lot more than even just sex. Her heart was involved; she felt it twist and splinter, jagged shards of disappointment digging into her soul. This was why she didn't believe in true love. This was why she didn't get involved with men she could care about. Until Ben.

How had he done it? Why had she let him?

On Saturday evening she'd broken down and rung Carlotta. She needed to talk to someone, someone who *knew* her. She felt a prickly, uncomfortable guilt in ringing her twin; she'd distanced herself from Carlotta since she'd had her son, Luca, five years ago. It had been an instinctive and unconscious decision, not that different from Ben pushing her off his lap, Natalia realised with a jolt. A means of self-protection. Carlotta's life had changed so dramatically, and hers hadn't. Carlotta had moved to Italy, had lived a quiet, sober life that Natalia secretly envied in its independence and freedom even as she witnessed Carlotta's heartbreak and sorrow.

Carlotta answered on the first ring. 'Natalia?'

'*Ciao*, Lotta.' The nickname from childhood slipped out instinctively.

Carlotta must have guessed something from her tone—or the nickname—for she asked quietly, 'Natalia, what's wrong?'

'Nothing,' Natalia said quickly. Her default was always to deny. It was so much easier that way, and she'd been doing it for so long. She knew what happened when you admitted weakness, gave in to fear. Shame followed, and humiliation.

Hurt and pain. She swallowed, the simple movement aching. 'Congratulations on your engagement.' Her sister's engagement to Prince Rodriguez—as well as Sophia's marriage to Ash—had been in the papers. Natalia hadn't read the articles, but she'd heard the details from her mother. Everyone was doing their royal duty, it seemed, except her.

She was falling for *exactly* the wrong kind of man.

'Natalia?' Carlotta questioned softly. 'Something is wrong. I can tell by your voice. What is it?'

'I...' Natalia closed her eyes, felt the pressure of tears behind her lids. So much was wrong. She felt the weight of everything—her own choices and failures, Ben's rejection, the hopelessness of her future—all of it pressing down on her, crippling her. How could she live with it all? How could she go on? 'I just wanted to talk to you,' she finally said. 'And see how you were doing.'

Carlotta was silent, and Natalia knew she hadn't fooled her sister. Weren't they twins? Didn't they sense each other's moods almost before the other even felt it? 'I'm fine,' she finally said.

'Are you really?' Natalia burst out. 'I mean...this marriage...'

'I'm only doing what we all must do,' Carlotta cut her off, her voice quiet and final. 'I'm more worried about you, Natalia. What is going on? We haven't spoken—'

'In years. I know.'

'Not *years*,' Carlotta said wryly.

'We haven't had a real conversation in years,' Natalia amended. She hadn't had a real conversation with anyone. Except Ben. And now she craved more of it, even as it frightened her. 'Carlotta,' she burst out suddenly, 'I just wanted to say I'm sorry for not being there when you had Luca. And after, I...' She swallowed, searched for words. 'I was afraid.'

'I know you were, Natalia.' She heard no condemnation in Carlotta's voice.

'And angry,' Natalia confessed in a whisper. 'About a lot of things. About how you were treated, and how it would change things. I felt like you were moving on to this whole new life without me.'

Carlotta let out a sad little laugh. 'I was, I suppose.'

'But I was selfish. I know that.'

'It was a long time ago.'

'Still. I just…wanted to be honest.' Even if it hurt. She wanted to change, and she didn't know how else to begin.

'What's going on, to provoke all this honesty?' Carlotta asked, a faint thread of humour in her voice.

'Nothing,' Natalia said quickly, and then let out a little laugh. So much for honesty. 'I've met someone,' she finally said. 'Someone who's challenged me.' As she spoke the words, she realised just how true they were. 'Someone's who's changed me,' she whispered. *And who hurt me.*

'Changed…?' Carlotta sounded surprised, but also happy. 'Are you engaged as well, Natalia?'

Engaged? 'No…' Of course Carlotta would jump to that conclusion. They'd always known they would marry men of their parents' choosing. Only last week her mother had shopped her in front of several dignitaries representing possible future husbands. How could she forget that even for a moment? It didn't matter what she felt for Ben. She had her royal duty. It didn't matter what Ben felt or thought—or what he didn't. They had no future.

'Natalia?' Carlotta prompted, interrupting her thoughts that swirled like leaves falling to the ground, withered, dry and dead. 'Who is this person?'

'Just someone,' she said, and the words sounded so final. So awful. She closed her eyes, felt fresh pain surge through her that almost sent her to her knees. 'Just someone,' she repeated in a whisper. 'No one important.' No one, she thought with an overwhelming ache of sorrow, who could be.

CHAPTER TEN

By Monday morning Natalia didn't feel any better inside, but at least she felt back in control. She'd taken care of her appearance, using all her hair and makeup tricks to disguise her reddened eyes and sallow complexion. Amazing what a weekend of moping did for your looks, she thought wryly as she applied bronzed blusher to her cheeks. She glanced in distaste at the sports shorts and T-shirt she would have to wear for a day on the football pitch. What she'd really like to wear, she thought, was her exclusively designed wrap dress in royal blue silk and a pair of four-inch heels. It would act as her armour; in it she'd be indestructible. Instead she was left with this useless PE kit.

By the time she arrived at the stadium, the children were already out on the pitch. Her gaze instinctively honed in on Ben's tall, lean form, and she watched as he demonstrated some incomprehensible maneuver to a cluster of rapt children. He called one boy out of the crowd: Roberto, a young, scruffy-looking boy of about ten whom Natalia had noticed had a natural athletic talent. He picked up the new move now with ease, and she saw Ben grin his approval. Her insides twisted unpleasantly. She didn't think Ben would be smiling much at her.

'You're late,' he told her a few minutes later. The children had divided into pairs and he'd come and found her at the registration table, where she was mindlessly organising pens and papers into neat piles.

'Traffic,' she said without looking at him. She'd hoped to gain some of her flirty confidence back when she saw him again, but it was too hard. All she could remember was the blazing look he'd given her before he'd pulled her to him and kissed her senseless. Tears stung behind her lids and she blinked them back furiously.

'Fine,' Ben said after a moment. 'Why don't you be goal-keeper?'

She jerked her gaze up. *'Goalkeeper?'* So kids could kick the ball at her all day? Was this Ben's warped idea of some-how getting her back for that kiss?

He raised his eyebrows in cool challenge. 'You have a problem with that?'

'Of course not,' Natalia said sweetly. How could she think she was falling in love with someone and want to stab his eye out with a pen at the same time? 'Why would I?' she asked him. She put the pen in the jar with the others. Taking a deep breath, she headed across to the goal area.

The next few hours were a test in both physical and emo-tional endurance. Although Natalia had improved her own football skills somewhat in the past week of volunteering, she wasn't yet adept enough to avoid getting hit repeatedly by the ball as she attempted to block it. The children cheered her on good-naturedly, and she forced herself to smile and laugh even though she was aching all over, inside and out. Ben didn't even look at her once.

By the end of the day all she wanted was a hot bath and a stiff drink. Unfortunately she had a state dinner with yet more dignitaries intent on sizing her up as a potential bride for some nameless royal. The thought only made her feel numb, for after a day of being virtually pummelled by shots on goal and Ben's blatant rejection she had no more emotional reserves to feel anything else.

She hurried out while Ben was giving his farewell pep talk, grateful that Enrico was waiting. She slipped into the sumptuous leather interior of the car and closed her eyes, thinking only that she didn't have to see Ben again until tomorrow.

She was wrong.

She'd just put the finishing touches on her makeup when she heard a knock on her bedroom door.

'Your Highness? Mr Jackson is downstairs.'

'Mr *Jackson*?' Natalia stared at her maid, Ana, in disbelief and more than a little dread. 'He's not expected.'

'He asked to see you. He had something to discuss.'

Natalia pressed her lips together. What on earth could Ben have to say to her? She felt a flutter of fear, and another more dangerous one of hope. Ridiculous. *Stupid.* 'Very well,' she said crisply. At least she was dressed appropriately this time. Her armour. She glanced down at the column dress of turquoise silk, a collar of diamonds at her throat. Taking a deep, calming breath she headed downstairs.

Ben paced the small, elegant salon he'd been directed to when he'd arrived unannounced at the palazzo. Although the sentries at the door had not betrayed a flicker of surprise or unease, Ben still sensed that he'd seriously disturbed royal protocol by arriving so suddenly.

'Their Royal Highnesses are hosting a dinner tonight,' the master butler had told him with a hint of reproach.

'This won't take a moment. I need to discuss a few things about the princess's volunteering duties,' Ben had replied tersely.

Actually, that was a lie. *Two* lies. He didn't know how long it would take, and he had no duties to discuss with Natalia. He didn't know what he was going to say, only that he'd come here on instinct, or maybe just need. After a day of doing his best to ignore Natalia and yet always remaining achingly, agonisingly aware of her, he knew he had to do something. Say something. Maybe even tell the truth.

Except he didn't even know what the truth was.

Ben let out a groan of angry frustration. Natalia had been right. He *was* scared. He hated feeling out of control, had organised his life so he never was. His childhood had been unsettled enough, with his parents together and then apart, his father with money and then without, the tabloids documenting every slip or stumble. Up and down, around and around, like a crazy out-of-control carousel, and Ben never felt like he knew what was going to happen.

Then he'd discovered football and thought he'd found a way to feel in control, to make his father and family proud. For a few short years he'd ridden that wave of success and accomplishment, and when it had been taken from him, he'd turned to business. He'd sought success and respect and he'd gained them. *Earned* them. And now he felt as if he were poised to lose it all, by falling in love with a woman who was beyond inappropriate, a woman with a history of scandals and affairs that rivalled his father's. What on earth was he thinking? He couldn't believe he'd even mentally formed the word *love*.

He didn't want love. Didn't trust it, didn't need it. And he was *not* in love with Princess Natalia.

'You wished to discuss something?'

Ben whirled around, blindsided by Natalia's sudden appearance. She looked every inch the regal princess in a turquoise silk evening gown that managed to be elegant and modest while still making his palms itch with the need to touch her. Her eyes glittered and her chin was lifted haughtily. She was on the defensive. Could he really blame her?

'I wanted to talk to you.'

She arched one eyebrow, coldly incredulous. 'I was with you all day, Ben. Is this really necessary?' With one golden, slender arm she indicated the palazzo and everything it represented. 'I'm afraid guests will be arriving at any moment.'

'This won't take long.'

She simply waited, leaving him tongue-tied. Damn. Why couldn't he think of a single thing to say? *Do?* He wanted to kiss her again. Desperately. If he did, would she push him away?

'Natalia…' he began. 'I'm sorry.' She said nothing, and he shifted his weight, unbearably uncomfortable, wishing he hadn't come. Natalia still didn't speak. Then he decided he needed to do what he'd done when he played football. As a striker, he'd always been a straight player, no tricks, no clever moves. Just honest skill, raw talent driving the ball towards the goal. And that's what he'd do now. 'I know I hurt you when I pushed you away from me in the airplane.'

'Fortunately I don't bruise easily.'

Frustration bubbled through him. He knew what she was doing. Like any good defender, she was keeping him from an easy, direct goal. Had he thought saying sorry would actually be enough? 'I didn't want to hurt you.'

She lifted her chin another notch. 'Like I said, you didn't.'

'You know that's not what I mean.' She said nothing, but he sensed her tension, felt it in himself. He felt his heart race the way it had when he was seconds away from a goal. 'I…I care about you, Natalia.'

She stilled, but her expression didn't change. 'Thank you,' she finally said, and Ben nearly had to keep his jaw from dropping in furious disbelief. *Thank you?* Definitely not the response he'd been going for. Hoping for. He felt like he did on the football pitch in an offside trap. He'd moved too far forward to attempt a goal and she'd moved back, leaving him offside and out of play. Useless. Vulnerable.

'I didn't expect to,' he continued, still trying to explain, to somehow redeem this conversation. 'I didn't want to.'

'That,' Natalia said coolly, 'is glaringly apparent.' She raised her eyebrows. 'Is that all you had to discuss? For as I said before, my guests will be arriving at any moment.'

Ben felt a slower anger start to burn inside him. All right, maybe it didn't sound like much, but he'd confessed more to this woman than he had to anyone else. He'd told her he cared and she'd said *thank you*.

He drew himself up, fury pounding like a pulse inside him. 'Yes,' he told her coldly, 'that's all.' And he strode out of the room without looking back.

Natalia stood very still as she listened to Ben's footsteps echo on the marble floor of the palazzo's foyer. If she moved, she felt she might break. *Shatter*. It had taken all her self-control, all her experience in acting the haughty, aloof princess, to play that role. To act like she didn't care.

And even now part of her wanted to wrench open the door and follow him through the palazzo, panting about how she cared too. And maybe even more than that.

No. She would not humiliate herself that way. She wouldn't take the paltry scraps Ben was offering. The realisation had grown in her as he'd stumbled through his awful nondeclaration. This was not what she wanted. It was not enough. If she was going to risk herself, all her vulnerabilities, then she wanted more. She wanted to be known, accepted, *loved*. The realisation stunned her even as it felt achingly, unbearably right. Yet Ben had barely been able to form the word *care*. And then those qualifiers: *I didn't expect to. I didn't want to.* Had he actually thought he was saying something she wanted to hear?

She let out a shuddering breath and slowly drew herself up, shoulders back, head tilted. A princess. And a woman, she knew now, who wanted love after all, in all of its fearful beauty and wondrous glory. Not someone who reluctantly, resentfully *cared*.

Not, Natalia reminded herself, that she would get either. She was about to meet the ambassador of Qadirah, a small island principality in the Arabian Sea, with a thirty-year-old bachelor sheikh and heir to the throne. A possible husband, and she'd never even met him. She didn't want to.

Walking stiffly, still aching, Natalia turned from the room.

The next day when Natalia arrived at the stadium the camp was in full swing, with Ben at its centre, working hard. She watched him run defense for Roberto, the boy he'd taken on as a young protegé. He was shouting instructions, sweat running down his face in rivulets. He looked amazing, but also angry. At least he had the football pitch to work out his frustrations. She'd had an interminable dinner with more veiled and not-so-veiled references to her salacious past, as well as a private conversation with the ambassador from Qadirah that had included a list of the sheikh's expectations for a bride. Submissiveness and discretion had figured prominently, not two of her best-known qualities. Natalia had barely slept all night, and her body still ached from yesterday's pummeling as goalie. Today was not going to be a good day.

Her fears were proved true just half an hour later, when a sudden cry sounded from the far side of the pitch and Natalia looked up to see a small knot of children and volunteers gathered around a fallen form. Her heart seemed to leap straight into her throat as she recognised the slight, scruffy figure. Roberto. Ben was bent over him, his face drawn and pale. Natalia knew immediately something very bad had happened.

Quickly she slipped out her mobile and dialed emergency services, requesting an ambulance. Then she hurried over to where Roberto lay fallen. One glance at the awkward angle of his leg told her that he had surely broken a bone. Ben looked up and caught sight of her and she saw a world of emotion in his dark eyes.

'What can I do?'

'Ring for an ambulance—'

'I did.'

Ben looked back down at Roberto, his face contorting in anxious worry and guilt, and Natalia came closer. The boy's face was pale and beaded with sweat, his teeth clenched. Natalia swept his silky fringe away from his forehead. *'Fa a un male cane, eh?'* she said with a small smile. It hurts like a dog. 'If it were me, I'd be screaming and crying. But then I'm not very good with pain.' Roberto didn't say anything, but he trained his pain-clouded gaze on her and Natalia kept speaking, barely knowing what she was saying, until she heard the wail of the ambulance's sirens in the distance.

Ben escorted Roberto to the ambulance, and as he climbed inside he gave Natalia a fleeting yet grateful smile.

'Thank you—'

'What about the rest of the camp?'

'I have to stay with Roberto,' Ben said. 'Can you manage?'

'Right—' Could she *manage*? A hundred children playing a sport she barely understood? Natalia straightened. 'Of course I can.'

The mood of the camp as she returned to the pitch was subdued, the children still gathered in anxious clusters. Natalia gave them all her most cheerful smile and clapped hands. 'Right. Everyone into a circle.'

She certainly couldn't coach football, and frankly after the harrowing events of the morning she thought everyone could use a bit of a break. 'Who knows how to play duck duck goose?' she asked cheerfully, and proceeded to explain how to play.

They spent the afternoon playing party games, to the children's delight and some of the volunteers' chagrin, and even though Natalia kept up a steady stream of cheerful encouragement she felt tired and tense, longing to know how Roberto—and Ben—were both doing.

When the camp was finally dismissed for the day, she helped to clean up and then asked Enrico to drive her to the island's main hospital, stopping on the way to pick up a few treats for Roberto. Ben wasn't there, but she found Roberto's parents waiting outside his room, looking tired and anxious. They stood, scrambling to attention as she approached them.

'Your Highness…'

'Scusi, scusi…'

She waved their protestations aside. 'We don't need to stand on formality here. How is Roberto?' She listened as they explained that he had indeed broken his leg, but it was a clean break and should heal. He'd be in plaster for six weeks, with physical therapy afterwards. She saw them both exchange anxious looks, and thought they were probably concerned about the cost. Santina had a national health-care system, but they would surely have to take time off work to care for their son. She realised with a jolt that they were wearing royal uniforms, and knew they must have jobs in the palazzo.

'Of course my father, King Eduardo, will want to help you with any costs associated with Roberto's injury,' she assured them, making a mental note to talk to her father about such a thing. She had no intention of making empty promises.

Roberto was asleep, but she left the basket of chocolate bars and comic books. Impulsively, as she got back in the car, she asked Enrico to drive her to the office.

Ben wasn't there, but Mariana was, clearing up for the day. 'Mr Jackson hasn't been in the office today,' she said when Natalia asked.

'Do you have his home address?'

If Mariana was surprised by such a request, she didn't show it. She looked it up on the computer and wrote it down, handing Natalia the paper. 'I don't know if he'll be home.'

'That's all right,' Natalia said with a breeziness she didn't really feel. 'I just wanted to talk to him about a few things.'

Back in the car again she gazed down at the written address, determined to still her hard-beating heart and make sense of the letters. She could do this. It just took time and concentration. 'Via Ventoso,' she finally told Enrico in triumph, and he started the car without a word.

Via Ventoso started in the city but then left the buildings behind for a stretch of empty road along the coast with only a few beach houses scattered among the rocks and palms. Enrico pulled into the shaded drive that led to Ben's house, a sprawling structure of glass and natural rough-hewn stone. Natalia slid out of the car and then, impulsively—for this whole evening had been an impulse—she told Enrico he could go.

The chauffeur hesitated. 'Are you certain, Your Highness?'

'Yes…I'll text you if you're needed. Thank you, Enrico.'

She waited until the limo had disappeared down the twisting road before she turned towards the house. It looked depressingly dark and empty. What on earth had she been thinking, coming here unannounced? Ben was probably out at some important business meeting and she'd just stranded herself, at least for a little while. She wasn't about to text Enrico five minutes after he'd left. She still had some pride.

She pressed the doorbell and listened to it echo through the house. She counted to ten, then twenty, and pressed it again. Counted again. Nothing.

Disappointment swamped her. *Why was she here?*

Desperately, and a little recklessly, Natalia turned the handle and to her surprise the door swung silently open. She stepped inside Ben's house, her heart surely beating loud enough for him to hear, wherever he was.

She came straight into the living room, a large, airy space with a few modern leather sofas and some rather stark contemporary art. The room was dark and empty, yet Natalia still saw a few small signs of Ben's presence: a pad of paper and a silver-plated pen on the glass coffee table, a paperback on the sofa. She crept closer and saw it was a rather light-hearted mystery. So Ben Jackson relaxed by reading a little fiction. The thought made her smile.

In the pristine kitchen she saw a coffee cup and cereal bowl washed and left on the dish drainer, and a bottle of vitamins by the sink, all fascinating glimpses into Ben's neat and rather stoic existence.

Hesitating, knowing she was being incredibly nosy, Natalia finally moved down the hallway that could only lead to the bedrooms. Two of the bedrooms were empty and unused; the third and last clearly belonged to Ben. Natalia's gaze swept the room but she could already sense it was empty. The king-size bed with its navy silk duvet had been made up with military precision. She saw some crumpled clothes in the corner, having missed the washing basket by about a metre, and a paperback by the bed. She crept closer and saw it was another light mystery. She smiled, imagined teasing him about his choice in reading material.

She peeked into the en suite bathroom, but it was also dark and empty. She saw a toothbrush, razor, a bar of shaving soap. The towels were hung to dry, the bath mat hanging off the edge of the tub. Ben, Natalia acknowledged without surprise, was a neat and rather Spartan man. He also wasn't home.

She walked back out into the living room, wondering where he was. What to do. She felt instinctively that he would not have left the door unlocked all day so he had to be nearby or else expecting to return soon. So should she wait? And why?

Just what was she doing here? What did she *want*?

Natalia pushed the uncomfortable questions aside and turned to stare moodily out at the white-sand beach that led right up to the sliding glass doors of the living room. Then with a jolt she saw that the door was partially ajar.

She slipped outside, kicking off her trainers that sunk into the sand. The sun was starting its descent towards the sea, streaks of vivid colour emblazoning the sky. Out here all Natalia could hear was the rattle of the wind in the palms and the gentle whoosh of the waves upon the sand.

As her eyes adjusted to the oncoming twilight, soft and

violet, she made out a cluster of palm trees, a few scattered boulders and then Ben, sitting alone on the beach with his head in his hands.

CHAPTER ELEVEN

B<small>EN</small> glanced up as Natalia approached, trepidation and compassion warring within her. He looked grave and perhaps even grim; was he displeased to see her? Natalia couldn't tell, yet she could certainly feel the depth of some nameless emotion rising from within him. His hooded gaze seemed to blaze through her senses and as she came to a halt a few metres away they stared at each other for a long moment, neither speaking.

Then Ben gave a strange, cynical little smile and Natalia braced herself for some cutting remark or command to leave. Instead he said, 'I've just been sitting here, thinking what a selfish bastard I am.'

Surprise flashed through her and she came to sit down next to him on the cool, hard sand. 'That doesn't sound like much fun.'

'No,' Ben agreed, turning back to stare straight ahead again at the darkening sea. 'It isn't.'

Natalia stared at the sea for a moment, trying to gather her scattered thoughts. 'Is it because of Roberto?' she finally asked.

'I was working him hard and I should have known better.'

'Known he would break his leg?' Natalia said with a lilt of wry disbelief. 'Because that's rather a difficult thing to know.'

'Know that a ten-year-old kid doesn't need to be a superstar,' Ben said flatly. 'Even if you want him to be. Even if you weren't.'

So this wasn't just about Roberto. 'You still couldn't have known, Ben. It was an accident. And accidents are out of your control.'

He let out a short, bitter laugh. 'Exactly.'

'What is that supposed to mean?'

She didn't think Ben was going to answer her. He remained silent, his gaze still on the sea, and then finally he spoke. 'I've spent my whole life trying to be in control of everything, to *feel* like I was in control. I told myself I was doing it for everyone's else sake—my family's or my mother's or whoever—but it was really for me.'

'I *told* you you were a control freak,' Natalia said lightly, but Ben didn't even smile. 'So did it work?' she finally asked quietly.

'Not really. Because I never was. Everything always spins out of control, every time.'

She certainly knew how that felt. 'You can't control other people's actions.'

'I haven't even controlled my own.'

Natalia felt her heart freeze for a suspended second. Was Ben talking about his actions with her? Kissing her? Surely not. She swallowed. 'So. Welcome to the club.'

'The club?'

'You don't think you're the only one who feels that way, do you?'

Ben let out of a bark of genuine laughter. 'You're not going to give me a shred of sympathy, are you?'

'Poor little princess?' Natalia reminded him. 'Nobody loves you? Nobody understands you?'

Ben gave her a sudden hard stare that sent awareness sizzling along her spine. 'I don't think that's true,' he said slowly, and it took Natalia a stunned moment to consider what he might mean. He understood her? He *loved* her?

'Of course it's not true,' she said briskly. 'Just like it's not true that you've ruined everyone's life including your own because of this obsessive and unhealthy need for control.'

He smiled. 'Obsessive? Really?'

'Why are you so concerned about being in control?' Natalia asked point-blank, without any humour or lightness in her voice to let Ben off the hook and deflect the question. She wanted to know the answer too much.

'Because I never felt like I had it,' he replied, his tone turning bleak. 'Everything about my life—my childhood at least—has been so up and down. So *crazy*. My mother divorced my father—twice. We moved from house to flat, one minute we were riding high and the next everything seemed a mess. My father was in the Premier League—'

'Like you wanted to be?' Natalia asked before she could stop herself, and Ben stared at her for a second.

'Yes.'

'You come alive on the football pitch like I've never seen before. You seem…happy.'

'I am,' Ben said quietly. 'At least, I was. I've always loved football. I was good at it—'

'And it was a way to feel in control.'

He shot her a wry glance. 'Yes.'

'So what happened?'

'I blew out my knee when I was seventeen. Lost any chance of playing professionally. My father was incredibly disappointed.'

How telling, she thought, that he talked about his dad's disappointment rather than his own. Natalia suspected Ben's ambition and need for control had been less for himself and more for his family and the stability of his many younger siblings.

'That must have been hard,' she said quietly, and he just shrugged.

'No one likes to lose a dream.'

'So then you went into business?'

He gave her the ghost of a smile. 'I had to do something, didn't I?'

Something to stay in control. Or at least feel like he was. Was that why he hated the press? she wondered. He couldn't control them. And yet she had chosen the opposite path... courting the newspapers and acting like she loved the attention because at least then she felt in control.

Yet all of it—any kind of control—was surely an illusion. She certainly wasn't in control when it came to Ben and her body's—as well as her heart's—elemental and overwhelming response to him. She stretched her toes out towards the water, now no more than a sound in the darkness. Night had fallen, soft and suggestive around them. Suddenly Natalia was very conscious that they were alone on a secluded beach, with only the stars to see them. She heard Ben's steady breathing, felt the heat and strength of his presence just inches from her.

'What about you, Princess?' Ben asked, his voice seeming almost disembodied in the darkness. 'What was your dream?'

Natalia tensed. She hadn't expected this to get personal... at least not about her. 'I don't know if I ever had one,' she said after a pause. 'Or at least I haven't, for a long time.'

'What did it used to be then?'

She took a breath, let it out slowly. He'd told her so much about himself, surely it was only fair she gave away a few of her secrets. She reached down and cupped a handful of cool, silky sand, letting it trickle between her fingers. 'I suppose it's rather predictable, something of the happily-ever-after variety.'

'Ah. So that's why you don't believe in true love.'

She smiled, remembering her disdainful remark. 'I've learned better.'

'What happened?'

'You can read all about it in the papers.' She felt rather than saw him tense.

'What do you mean?'

'That torrid affair. You mentioned it yourself. It was big news about six years ago.' Right before Carlotta had fallen pregnant and trumped Natalia's own shame.

He didn't speak for a moment, and Natalia could almost imagine the wheels turning in his mind, the click of the cogs. 'The French guy?'

'Jean, yes. He was a count's son, I believe. He spent the summer on the island.'

'And what happened? He broke your heart?'

'It felt like it at the time.' She shrugged, not wanting to rake up old memories, old hurts. 'I thought I was in love and I did a lot of stupid things and he told them all to the tabloids. Gave them photos.' She closed her eyes briefly, remembered the scorching shame of seeing what she'd thought had been a wonderful and private romance laid bare in all of its humiliating detail. 'He got a lot of money for it anyway,' she finished lightly. 'It was an exclusive.'

'I'll bet.' Ben shook his head. 'So that wasn't your choice.'

'No.'

'The papers made it seem like it was.'

She shrugged as if it didn't matter. 'That's what papers do.'

Ben gave her a hard look. 'And so after that you decided you'd be the one calling the shots. You'd go to them before they could get you.'

He'd summed it up so perfectly, yet she thought she heard a thread of judgement in his voice. 'Something like that.'

He let out a huff of breath. 'And I did the opposite.' Was he implying that's what she should have done? And maybe she should have. Lived life quietly, above reproach, like Carlotta had. Like Ben had. Surely it was too late now for regrets. But was it too late to change? To *want* to change?

'When I was young,' Ben said slowly, 'about four or five, the papers printed a photograph of me. I was crying. I'm not sure if it had to do with my parents' divorce or not. Maybe I'd just skinned my knee and some photographer got the shot.

In any case, that blasted photo was in every newspaper from here to Los Angeles. My mother hated it, made her feel like her privacy had been invaded, like the world was watching the breakdown of her marriage and its effect on her children. I hated it because what boy wants the world to see him crying?'

Natalia gave him a glimmer of a smile. 'No boy that I can think of.'

'And there were others. It seemed like every unguarded moment of my childhood was captured on film and tied to my parents' marriage. All I had to do was look a little glum and the papers were screaming about how my mother's heart was broken.'

'That must have been hard for her.'

'It was.'

'And you.' He shrugged, and she continued quietly, 'And when you injured your knee? They must have had a field day.'

'You saw those photos?'

She laughed softly, yet without humour. 'No. I just know how the press works. They blow everything out of proportion. Use everything they can get.'

He nodded. 'It was tough.'

She sighed, feeling sad for both of them. Their experiences had been so similar, yet their responses so incredibly different.

'Your hatred of the press is starting to make sense. Not to mention your control issues.'

'But both of those things have blinded me.'

'Blinded you?'

'To the way things really are.' He paused, his gaze hard, unyielding, relentless. She could not look away from it. 'To the way you really are.'

Natalia felt her heart freeze, suspended in her chest, before it seemed to do a free fall. This was what it was to be known. Except Ben didn't really know her. Not all of her.

Stupid, slow Natalia.

She angled her head away from him. 'Don't go overboard on me, Ben,' she said lightly, although her voice sounded strangled to her own ears. 'I'm not that different from what I seem.' Her heart hammered insistently otherwise. *Yes, I am, yes, I am.* Why was she pushing him away? Was it just fear? If she pushed him away first, he wouldn't get the chance. Just like with the tabloids, with everyone, even Carlotta. Act-attack-first, and you wouldn't get hurt.

'Aren't you?' Ben said quietly, and she felt his hand on her jaw, turning her to face him. She opened her mouth to say something, something sharp and cutting, but no words came out. Ben's eyes blazing into her own, scorched her soul. She was on fire, and no more so than when he leaned forward and kissed her.

This kiss was so different from the others. His lips brushed hers, once, twice, like a greeting. Then slowly, deliberately, he deepened the kiss, his lips parting, the tip of his tongue sweetly demanding her own to part, and a soft sigh of surrender escaped her without her even realising it.

Ben reached up to cradle her cheek with his hand, his thumb brushing her jawbone, the movement so achingly tender tears came to Natalia's eyes. His mouth moved more surely over hers, taking, demanding, *needing*, and the sweetness fell away to reveal the hunger underneath.

She heard his breath release in a ragged gasp that matched her own as he eased her back on the sand, one knee nudged between her legs, his hand sliding under her T-shirt, his palm warm on her bared skin.

Her T-shirt…even in her passion-dazed state Natalia realised she was grubby and muddy and wearing PE kit. Not exactly the setting for a seduction. But this wasn't a seduction. This was need, maybe even love. And it didn't matter what she wore or looked like, because they were both beyond that.

The realisation of how much this meant to her slammed into her, left him more dazed than ever. Ben must have sensed something of it for he drew back, his dark eyes glittering as he gazed down at her.

'Natalia…?' Her name was a question.

'Yes…' she whispered, because the thought of stopping now—even if it was sensible, strong, *safe*—was surely impossible. She needed this too much. She needed Ben.

Ben kissed her again, like a brand or a seal, and then he rose from the beach. 'We're doing this properly.'

'Properly…?' Natalia repeated uncertainly, for part of her wanted passion, hard and quick, right there on the beach. Anything else—anything more—felt too scary. Too much.

Ben just smiled, and lacing her fingers with his own, he led her back to the beach house, and his bedroom with that huge king-size bed. Natalia stared at the slippery-smooth sheets with a flicker of uncertainty. Doubts crept in.

'I'm dirty,' she said, gesturing to her muddy clothes, and he drew her closer, shaking his head.

'You're perfect.'

But she wasn't perfect, Natalia thought. She'd made so many mistakes, had so many problems and weaknesses and flaws. Ben didn't even know them all. And she couldn't forget, even now, that he'd pushed her off his lap when he thought someone might see. Had that moment been a real reflection of his feelings—or was this one?

'Natalia. Look at me.'

She realised she'd been scrunching her eyes shut and she opened them, stared into his face. He looked as calm and steady as ever, and she wanted to trust him. She wanted to love him.

'Do you want this?' Wordlessly she nodded. 'Why are you afraid?'

Her throat felt so tight she could barely speak. 'Because this is scary.'

Ben gave her the glimmer of a smile. 'You've got that right,' he said, and he kissed her again, a hard press of his lips against hers that felt like a promise. 'Perhaps,' he suggested as his hands slid underneath her T-shirt, 'we shouldn't overthink it.'

She nodded, even as her brain buzzed with the feel of his hands on her skin, cool and so assured. So knowing. She didn't want to think. Thinking meant doubt, uncertainty, fear. She just wanted to feel. 'Sounds good to me,' she murmured, and slid her arms around his neck, drawing him closer, pulling his face down to hers so their lips met again in a desperate, demanding kiss. The kind of kiss that would obliterate any thought at all.

Ben stilled, pulled away. 'I didn't mean for you to completely shut off your mind,' he said wryly, and frustration bubbled within her.

'Is *everything* with you a lesson?' she demanded, and he laughed softly.

'I just want you to know what you're doing. This is a *decision*. It's me you're making love to, Princess.'

Natalia widened her eyes, gave her voice its familiar mocking edge. '*What* was your name again?' she asked, but Ben didn't smile. He looked so serious, so *intent*.

'Don't do that,' he said quietly. 'Don't make this a mockery. Don't put yourself down. You're worth more than that, Natalia.'

Tears stung her eyes and she blinked them back furiously, looking away. 'Am I?' she asked, the words torn from her raw, aching throat. A tear spilled down her cheek. She hadn't meant to say that. Feel that. And she certainly hadn't wanted to reveal it to Ben.

'Yes,' he said softly, 'you are.' He wiped away her tear with his thumb, his hands cradling her face. 'And I'm going to show you how much.'

His gaze steady on her, he laid her on the bed, gently yet with purposeful determination. There was no question about who was in charge here. She was most definitely not calling the shots.

And it made her feel more afraid and vulnerable than ever.

'What are you doing?' she asked in an unsteady whisper.

'Loving you.'

Ben slid his T-shirt off and tossed it in the corner. The sight of his bare, sleekly muscled chest left Natalia breathless. When his shorts followed, she felt almost dizzy. He was really a most beautiful man.

Loving you.

Did he really mean that? Was she dreaming? Even now her body tensed, both in expectation and fear. She wanted this, but she was still so afraid. Afraid of being hurt. Of being rejected. Again. *Always.*

Ben stretched out alongside her, pressing a kiss to her jaw, his stubble rasping her cheek, his hand sliding up under her T-shirt to cup her breast. 'First of all,' he murmured, 'we need to get rid of these clothes.'

Natalia couldn't agree with him more, yet she still felt exposed when Ben drew them off her himself, his hands sliding all the way down her legs as he took off her shorts, then up her torso and breasts as he divested her of her T-shirt. Now they were both naked.

She'd been naked before with a man. She'd slept with several men, one she'd thought she loved. But it had never felt like this. Not even close. When Ben looked at her, his gaze sweeping slowly over her from the crown of her head to the tips of her toes, she felt as if he were seeing into her soul. *Knowing* her.

She blushed. All over. 'I go blotchy when I blush,' she whispered, and thoughtfully Ben pressed a finger to the rosy stain across her chest.

'So you do.' He bent and pressed a kiss to the same spot. 'Intriguing.'

She squirmed. Why was this so uncomfortable? Even with

desire pooling inside her, coursing through her veins, she felt too exposed. Too afraid.

Maybe she didn't want to be known after all.

Ben lifted his head to gaze all too understandingly at her. 'You're thinking.'

'You didn't want me to turn off my brain.'

'Turn it down a notch then, Princess. Stop thinking something bad is going to happen.'

'I'm not—' She struggled for words, for breath. 'I'm not used to this.'

'I know.'

'Really?' She couldn't keep herself from attacking, even now, when they were naked, their bodies pressed so intimately together, Ben looking at her so tenderly. 'I've been with plenty of men before, you know. The tabloids didn't get it that wrong.' She was exaggerating on purpose, to push him away. Even now. Especially now.

Ben gazed at her steadily. 'This is nothing like that.'

Natalia felt as if he'd stolen the breath right from her lungs. 'That's why I'm so scared,' she whispered.

'And you think I'm not?' Ben asked, his voice a raw whisper. 'I'm scared, and as you pointed out, I'm scared of *being* scared. I've got it double. So I beat you in that department, Princess.'

She laughed, a bubble of joy rising inside her, relaxing her, and Ben bent his head to her body, his mouth moving over her breasts, sucking, nipping. She threaded her fingers through his hair, so crisp and soft, as sensation took over. She definitely wasn't overthinking this now.

Yet Ben never let her slide into oblivion. Any time she did, closing her eyes, throwing her head back, *forgetting*, he brought her back to the present, to him, nudging her eyes open, making her respond not just with her body, but with her mind. Her heart.

She writhed underneath him, resisting, wanting this to be simple. Easy. Safe.

Yet nothing about being with Ben was any of those things. It was frightening and wonderful and far too intense. His mouth moved down her body, lingering in certain places, his tongue tasting her skin, *memorising* her. Natalia lay there, accepting and strangely humbled, and yet also fighting the tide of desire that threatened to wash right over her, sweep her out to sea. She was afraid of this. Afraid of losing control, of being laid bare, body and heart and mind, before him.

His hair brushed her tummy as he moved lower, and then his mouth was between her legs, right at the centre of her, and Natalia tensed. His hands rested on her thighs, gently forcing her to stay splayed, utterly exposed and vulnerable, everything open to him, and she couldn't bear it.

Natalia tried to pull away, resisting, afraid and embarrassed, but Ben wouldn't let her hide herself. His mouth pressed against her and her body jerked in response, pleasure and sensation spiralling upwards inside her as her voice caught on a jagged cry. His tongue flicked against her folds and she cried again, the pleasure so intense it felt painful.

Still she resisted, her hips twisting as she tried to free herself from his hands. 'Don't—' she gasped, and yet when he stopped she felt as if a jagged hole had been cut through her; she was devastated, empty and aching.

'Don't fight it, Natalia. Don't fight *me*.'

'I can't—' she gasped, because even now the thought of him seeing her like this made her want to cringe and hide.

'Why?' Ben asked quietly. She felt his breath feather her heated skin. 'Why can't you?'

'Because...'

His hands rested on her thighs, steady and warm. 'Do you want me to stop?'

'No—' she gasped, because *that* thought was intolerable. His mouth found her again and this time Natalia couldn't resist it. She gave herself up to the feeling, to *him*, and when she cried out, her voice a broken splinter of sound, he slid inside her, *consuming* her as tears of both emotional and physical release streamed down her face and pleasure like nothing she'd ever known coursed through her, filled her heart to overflowing so the shell around it cracked and broke right open.

Her body clenched around him and she matched him stroke for stroke, tears still streaking down her face, waves of pleasure washing over her in an endless tide. Then she felt Ben find his own release, his body shuddering against hers before he subsided, their hearts beating a desperate rhythm against each other.

She was completely exposed, her body *and* heart, and there was nothing she could do about it. No way to hide or pretend now. Gently Ben wiped the tears from her face as her body shuddered in the aftermath of the most intense orgasm she'd ever experienced.

Her heart felt like something fragile and fledgling, exposed to the elements, barely able to survive. Even now she wanted to pull away and protect it. Protect herself.

He kissed the corner of her eye where another tear had started to trickle down. 'Are these good tears?' he murmured.

'I don't know,' Natalia confessed in a shaky whisper. 'I don't know what they are.' She'd never felt so much. Revealed so much. She felt both empty and full at the same time.

Ben didn't answer, but as he rolled off her Natalia felt ridiculously bereft, as if he'd just left her. Rejected her. He slipped from the bed and she watched in surprise and then understanding as he moved through the darkness of the bedroom. He turned on the light in the en suite bathroom and a second later he slid back into bed and pulled her towards him. He fit her snugly against him, his chin resting on her shoulder as his thumb continued to trace the silvery track of tears down her cheek.

'Better?' he whispered, and she nodded, felt herself slowly

start to relax, the tightly held parts of herself loosen. They had been good tears after all. 'Happy?' he asked, and she smiled and reached for his hand, threading his fingers with her own.

'Yes,' she said. 'Happy.' And safe. In Ben's arms, she felt safe *and* vulnerable, which was a mind-blowing combination. She felt known.

And it was wonderful.

CHAPTER TWELVE

NATALIA woke slowly to sunlight, her body aching in the most amazing places. She shifted, felt Ben's arm heavy across her and smiled. Memories of last night drifted through her mind in pleasure-splintered fragments, memories of an intimacy so incredible and life-changing she could hardly believe it was real. It had happened.

She turned so she could see Ben, his face relaxed in slumber, his lashes long and curly on his stubble-roughened cheeks. Still smiling she reached over and with one finger touched his mouth, the mouth that had kissed and loved her all over. Even now, in the safety of his embrace, the memories made her blush. This was all so new, not just Ben, but her. Who she was. Who she was with him.

Ben opened his eyes and blinked sleep from them before giving her a lazy smile. 'Princess,' he said, 'are you checking me out?'

'No—' Natalia said instinctively, and his smile deepened.

'You shouldn't have told me how you go blotchy. I can tell when you're lying.' He pressed one finger to the now-rosy skin of her throat. Natalia let out a reluctant laugh.

'All right, so I might have been checking you out,' she said, staying flippant. 'So what?'

'I like it,' he told her, and nuzzled her neck. 'I like it a lot.'

'Don't get all arrogant on me now,' she said, and Ben lifted his head to gaze at her steadily.

'Trust me, Natalia, you keep me humble.'

She swallowed, moved by the sincerity on his face. In his eyes. He'd let go, she realised. He wasn't letting the fear or lack of control keep him back, yet she still felt uncertain. Afraid. And she knew that wasn't fair to him. Tentatively she touched his cheek. 'I like it when you say my name,' she whispered.

'I like that you like it,' he said, his eyes darkening, and then he captured her mouth in a consuming kiss. They didn't speak any more for a little while.

Later, as she showered in Ben's en suite bathroom while he saw to breakfast, Natalia heard himself humming. Felt herself smiling. Had she ever been this happy before? Had she ever felt this free, this loved?

Ben hadn't said it, not really. *Loving you.* Last night had he simply meant physically, or something more? She could hardly ask for clarification of that statement. Yet she felt, with a fragile hopefulness, that he did love her. That last night he'd been showing he loved her, in so many ways.

But he doesn't really know you.

The whisper slid slyly into her mind, filled it with the slow, seeping poison of doubt. Natalia stilled, tensed, the water from the shower still streaming over her. She knew she still had secrets, things she hadn't told Ben, important things. And with that hidden knowledge came a lingering fear that this couldn't last. It couldn't actually be real. He'd tell her he'd changed his mind or he'd discover something that would *make* him change his mind….

How could she trust him? She didn't *do* trust. She'd learned at all of five years old that you didn't show your weaknesses. You didn't tell people your fears. Yet she'd been doing just that ever since she'd met Ben. Something in him—that quiet, rocklike core of steadiness—made her want to tell him. To reveal herself, even as she kept retreating and trying to cover her tracks. Cover herself.

Natalia leaned her head against the slippery tile and closed her eyes as the water streamed over her like tears. She didn't know if she could do this. If she was brave enough to be honest, strong enough to be vulnerable.

Why does it have to be so hard?

She had no answer.

As Natalia came out of the bathroom, swathed in a huge terrycloth towel, she saw that Ben had laid out a clean T-shirt and shorts of his to wear. Natalia slipped them on, grabbing one of his belts to cinch at her waist for the clothes swam on her. Not the most fashionable of outfits, but it touched her that Ben had thought of it at all.

She followed the mouthwatering aroma of bacon and eggs frying to the kitchen, where Ben stood by the stove, dressed in a pair of faded jeans and a worn grey T-shirt. Even now the sight of him, from his rumpled hair to his bare feet, made her mouth dry and her heart thud.

She loved him. She wanted to love him…if she'd let herself.

Why does it have to be so hard?

'Hey.' Her throat felt scratchy, her voice wobbly and she tried again. 'That smells good.'

Ben glanced up, his eyes glinting as he took in her appearance. 'I like your new look.'

She held out her arms, the T-shirt sliding off one shoulder. 'They're a little big.'

'You look gorgeous.' And she knew he meant it. Why was he being so *nice*? Natalia wondered. She was waiting for the sting. She was *always* waiting for it. She glanced away, anywhere but at him. 'Coffee?' Ben asked, and when she nodded he handed her a steaming mug which she took with murmured thanks, wrapping her hands around its comforting warmth.

She cleared her throat. 'So.'

Ben glanced at her, amusement quirking his mouth and lightening his eyes. 'So,' he repeated, and inwardly she started to squirm.

'This isn't easy.'

'No?' He took a sip of coffee, watching her over the rim of his mug.

'I'm not…' She took a breath, let it out slowly. 'I'm not really used to this.'

'I'm not either.'

She pursed her lips. 'Why do you seem so relaxed then?'

He paused, seeming to weigh his words carefully. 'Because last night made me happy.'

'It made happy too,' Natalia muttered. She could feel herself starting to blush again. *Wonderful.*

Ben smiled. 'I know it did.'

'I think your eggs are burning,' she told him, and felt a rush of relief when he turned back to the stove. She was so not ready for this kind of honesty. Intimacy. It was entirely out of her experience, totally foreign to the way she normally operated. Defend. Deflect. Go on attack. Anything to keep people from getting close. From knowing.

She took a sip of coffee and wandered over to the sliding glass doors that led to the beach. The sunlight sparkled off the water, and she could see both her and Ben's footprints in the sand, leading back to this door. Upstairs. Memories of last night rushed through her again and her throat tightened, her fingers clenching around the mug. Desire and dread, hope and fear, warred within her, an impossible tangle of emotions.

'Breakfast is ready,' Ben said, and she turned to see he'd placed two plates loaded up with eggs and bacon on the glass-topped table.

'Fabulous.' She wasn't sure she could manage a mouthful, but she came to the table with her gamest smile. Not that she could ever fool Ben.

'And I thought we could read the papers,' Ben continued, smiling as he dropped two well-reputed papers on the table. 'No paparazzi photographs, I promise.'

Natalia stilled, stared at those newspapers. Such a simple

little thing. Reading the papers over coffee and eggs, sharing bits of news and toast with each other. What normal people did. What everyone else did. And virtually impossible for her.

'Natalia?' Ben prompted. She looked up, saw him frowning at her and she felt the pressure build in her chest.

It should be so easy to tell him. It *could* be. She knew he would show her compassion rather than contempt; she knew him—loved him—well enough to believe that. Yet she still couldn't form the words. Bare her secret, her soul. It was just too hard. And she didn't want to have him look at her with pity, couldn't bear that now when she was already feeling so exposed and vulnerable.

'What's wrong?' he said quietly and Natalia shook her head.

'I can't do this.'

'Do what? Eat breakfast?' He kept his voice light. 'Read the paper?'

Yes. 'All of it. This…playing at some kind of happy families. Being a couple. I can't do it.'

Ben's expression hardened even though she knew he was trying to stay reasonable. In control. As always. 'Why not?'

'I know it's easy for you, Ben—'

'It's not actually.'

'You seem to have fallen into the role of attentive boyfriend rather easily,' Natalia snapped, and Ben's eyes flashed temper.

'You think it comes naturally, Natalia? You think I'm not *trying*? Because just like you, I've avoided relationships. Commitment. I've seen the train wreck of my parents' marriage and I haven't wanted anything like it. I'm still wary. Still *afraid*.' His voice throbbed with both sincerity and anger and he let out a shuddering breath. 'But I recognise that we have something between us—something I've never had with anyone else—and think I'd keep at it, see if it works. Why aren't you?'

'Because it won't.' The pressure in her chest was taking

over her whole body, so every muscle and nerve ached with suppressed emotion. Something had to happen or she'd surely explode. 'It can't.'

'You're so sure about that, Princess?'

'Yes, Ben, I am.' She kept her voice cutting, as sharp as it ever was, a razor of remembrance that cut through the emotion, reminding them both of who they were and where they'd started. 'Because I'm a princess, just like you said. And we don't have a *relationship*, because—' She took a breath, made herself make the final cut. 'I'm about to marry someone else.'

She saw Ben draw back as if she'd punched him. For a second he looked shocked, devastated, and then he blinked, and the expression was wiped clean from his face. Natalia felt her breath come out in a tearing gasp and she stared back at him, her whole body taut and quivering with tension. 'I see,' he finally said, his voice utterly devoid of feeling. 'I'm afraid I didn't realise that.' He sounded horribly, eerily polite, and Natalia just stood there as he nodded towards the door. 'There's not much else to say then, is there?'

'No,' she agreed, her voice a scratchy whisper. Yet words clambered inside her, clogged in her throat. There was so much more to say. It was just she was so afraid to say it.

Ben nodded again towards the door, a dismissal. Still trembling, her chin held high, Natalia walked towards the front door. She saw he'd left her trainers lined up neatly by the door, next to his, a small yet achingly painful thoughtfulness, and she blinked back tears. She imagined, for one blinding second, how things could be different. She imagined her sweater tossed carelessly on a chair, her shampoo and makeup scattered over his Spartan sink. Her *life* here. Her here.

Then, without looking at him, she reached for the trainers and slipped them on. Ben didn't say anything. After an endless moment when her fingers fumbled with the laces she finally straightened, opened the door and walked out of his life.

Ben stood in the centre of the dining room, the front door

closing a final-sounding click that echoed through his heart. She'd left. She'd just…left.

And she was getting married.

What the hell…?

Ben raked his hands through his hair, stared in uncomprehending disbelief at the two plates of breakfast, the coffee, the papers. He'd envisioned a relaxed, enjoyable morning; he'd anticipated being real—being normal—with Natalia. He'd wanted that. He'd wanted that so much.

You seem to have fallen into the role of attentive boyfriend rather easily.

Shame and fury churned in his gut, pulsed through his blood. He *had* fallen into that role, a role he'd never wanted or envisioned for himself. A role he'd disdained. And yet with Natalia he'd been all too ready to imagine a life—a love— with her. It felt humiliatingly ridiculous. She hadn't had any intention of taking what happened between them beyond last night…and he'd been picturing fairy tales. Happy endings. A *relationship*. His behaviour reminded him of his mother's, always eager and willing to forgive. Willing to try again.

He wouldn't be like that. He couldn't.

And he wouldn't even be given the opportunity. Natalia was getting married.

In one abrupt movement Ben cleared the plates from the table, dumped the eggs in the bin. Even these cleansing actions felt shameful, humiliating. How many meals had his mother made that his father hadn't eaten? How many evenings had she waited for him, and he'd stumbled in late, drunk and smelling of another woman's perfume? He loved his father; he'd forgiven the man his weaknesses, but that didn't mean he'd *ever* intended to be like his mother.

And yet here he was, alone, abandoned, his heart aching.

No. His heart had nothing to do with this.

I'm about to marry someone else.

He couldn't believe it. He couldn't believe in all the time

he'd known her, she'd forgotten to mention such a relevant and important detail. It felt like a lie. He knew, of course, that her parents were intent on lining up spouses for all the Santina siblings. He would have expected, if he'd allowed himself to think of it, that they might have someone in mind for Natalia. The papers had been full of her broken engagement to a prince of some small European principality.

The papers.

Why hadn't the newspapers, the tabloids, mentioned anything about Natalia's forthcoming marriage? Why hadn't King Eduardo announced it at Allegra's party three weeks ago? Why had he never heard a whisper of it all this time?

Because it wasn't real. It wasn't happening. Not yet anyway.

His breath released in a shuddering rush as realisations clicked into place. Natalia had *told* him this wasn't easy for her. He knew she was afraid. He understood that last night had been both wonderful and frightening for her, that the vulnerability of even an orgasm had shaken her.

And when she'd snatched the first excuse she could to allow her to walk out of here, he, frightened *fool* that he was, had believed her.

Ben straightened and smiled grimly. Natalia wasn't going to get off that easily. Not by a long shot.

She hadn't thought through things. Natalia realised that as soon as she returned back to the palazzo, having texted Enrico to pick her up. The chauffeur didn't pass any judgements, but she could tell something was going on. Something was wrong.

So much was wrong. She leaned her head against the seat and closed her eyes, exhaustion and misery swamping her. She saw Ben's shocked face in her mind's eye and felt a rush of guilt as well. Yet she'd spoken the truth. She *was* going to be married, if not quite as soon as she made out. This thought only added to her unhappiness.

Yet the fact that she'd only told him about her possible marriage because she'd been afraid of what was happening between them needled her, burrowed under her skin, a jagged splinter that she could not ignore or remove.

She felt the tension snap through the air as soon as she entered the palazzo. One of her mother's staff swooped down on her as soon as she arrived, informing her that Queen Zoe requested her presence immediately.

Natalia hurried to her bedroom and changed into a mint-green linen dress and matching high-heeled espadrilles. She could hardly face her mother in Ben's T-shirt and shorts... even if she couldn't resist pressing them to her face, as if she could still catch the faint scent of him, before dropping them determinedly in the corner of the room.

'*Where* have you been?' Queen Zoe demanded icily as Natalia entered her room.

'I'm sure Enrico told you,' Natalia replied. She was surprised at how calm she felt. Her confrontation with Ben had sapped all of her emotional reserves. He'd taken everything.

'He said,' Zoe informed her, 'that he drove you to Mr Jackson's house.'

'Yes.'

'And you returned to the palazzo this *morning*.'

Natalia met her mother's narrowed gaze evenly. 'Yes.'

'Natalia, this behaviour...' Her mother shook her head, her outrage turning to genuine distress. 'It must stop.'

'It has,' Natalia said, even though she knew she and her mother were really talking about completely different things. 'It's over.'

'Because,' Queen Zoe continued, her voice hardening once more, 'the Sheikh Prince of Qadirah has made an official offer. He is arriving this week to arrange the contractual details. As soon as those are settled, your marriage will be announced.'

* * *

Somehow Natalia dragged herself through the next few days. She kept mostly to her room, avoiding the flurry of activity the imminent arrival of the Prince of Qadirah seemed to cause. She tried not to think of Ben, but her mind—and body—betrayed her, both remembering how sweetly he had kissed her. Loved her.

And if she'd only had a little more courage she could have stayed. She'd have told him everything, and maybe…maybe they could have worked something out.

She knew the thought was foolish, the hope vain. She was about to be *married*. Even if she'd stayed, even if she'd trusted Ben, they would only have had a few more hours at best. A single morning. And maybe not even that.

Even if she wasn't getting married, Natalia reminded herself, Ben had never actually said he'd loved her. *I recognise that we have something between us—something I've never had with anyone else—and I'm willing to keep at it, see if it works*. Not exactly a promise to build a dream on. A life on. What if he had decided it wasn't working? What if this time he didn't push her off his lap, but out of his life?

Perhaps, Natalia told herself as she prepared to go to camp on Monday morning, this was better. It was certainly safer. A marriage with the Sheikh of Qadirah would be cordial, convivial perhaps, but they would essentially lead separate lives, especially once she'd provided an heir. That much had been made clear to her by the ambassador. There would be no intimacy, no vulnerability, no *knowing*. And that, she told herself resolutely, was a good thing. Even if it didn't feel like it was.

By the time Natalia arrived at camp a few days later she'd pushed all these thoughts away, had blanked her mind and her heart. It was surely the only way to get through the day.

Ben was busy on the pitch when Natalia arrived at the stadium. She made sure to keep away from him, helping out at the registration table, not looking at him as he issued orders. Perhaps she could get through this day without actually talking to him. The thought brought both sorrow and relief.

Of course she should have known Ben would never let her off so easily. He called her to him at the centre of the pitch late in the morning, the children gathered all around.

'Princess Natalia and I will demonstrate how to guard the goal,' Ben said in his careful Italian, a football in his hands. 'An important skill, no matter what position you are playing. Sometimes in a match the goalkeeper is injured and another player has to substitute, so it's always worth knowing how to do it.' He nodded towards Natalia. 'Princess Natalia will act as goalkeeper first.'

Fabulous. Just about the last thing she wanted was Ben kicking the football straight at her. Her head held high, Natalia marched towards the goal area and turned to face Ben. His face was grimly set, his eyes blazing determination, and she braced herself for a hard kick aimed at her head.

She should have known better than that. She should have known *Ben* better than that. He punted a soft kick straight to her feet, ridiculously simple for even her to trap.

'Now that's not going to happen too often,' Ben told the children with a smile. 'When players want to score a goal, they're going to kick hard. They're going to give it everything they've got, and you have to brace yourselves for that.' He turned back to Natalia, and she tensed. 'Ready?' he asked her, and tersely she nodded.

He kicked the ball hard, but not too hard. With taut effort she was able to keep it from getting in the goal. Ben turned back to the children. 'Now Princess Natalia really wants to keep me from scoring,' he said with a smile, although Natalia detected a slight edge to his voice. 'But sometimes, when a football is coming straight at you, and all you can see is that hard and fast-moving ball, you're scared. That's understandable. You're afraid to commit to the maneuver.'

Natalia tensed again. She had a feeling Ben was talking

about something more than football. Something a whole lot more personal. He raised his voice so every child could hear. So she could hear. 'That's when you've got to be brave,' he said. 'That's when you've got to give this game everything you've got.'

Tears stung Natalia's eyes. She hadn't been brave. She'd been so afraid, but it was too late. The game was over for them, even if Ben didn't realise it.

'Now,' Ben said, 'it's my turn. Princess Natalia will kick the ball to me.' As he passed her the football, he murmured, 'Kick it to the outside post, if you can.'

Natalia had no idea what he was getting at now, but she nodded. She thought she could manage that. She turned to face Ben, saw him prepare for the kick, his muscular body taut and achingly beautiful.

'Sometimes,' he said, his gaze fastened to hers, boring into her soul, 'you've got to let yourself really go. More than you ever would. More than you want to.' He nodded at her, and she kicked the ball to the corner of the goal.

Ben dived for it, the extension elegant and total, his body nearly parallel to the ground, his arms outstretched. He was completely committed to the dive. Everyone watched in awe as he caught the ball and fell to the ground, landing on his shoulder and side before rolling into a sitting position. He turned to the crowd of children with a triumphant smile.

'You see? I didn't even get hurt. At least, not more than a little.' His gaze moved to Natalia, settled on her with unmistakable emphasis. 'But it was worth it.'

CHAPTER THIRTEEN

NATALIA didn't talk to Ben for the rest of the day, but his words raced through her mind, churned in her gut. *You're afraid to commit. That's when you've got to be brave. That's when you've got to give this game everything you've got.*

He'd been talking to her, she knew it. Talking about them. And maybe she should have been braver. Maybe she could have given more. It didn't matter now. It was too late. In a few days her marriage would be announced. Natalia took a deep breath. She knew it was too little, too late, but at least she could be honest with Ben now. Even if it couldn't change things.

She waited until the children were trickling away, the stadium empty and silent. Natalia moved around the pitch gathering all the footballs that had rolled too far away for anyone to bother with. She put them all in the net bag and then dragged it over to the folding table where Ben stood, frowning at some papers there.

'Ben,' she said quietly, and he tapped what she saw was a newspaper.

'Read that.'

Funny, how easy it was after all this time, to tell him her secret. Strange how it really didn't matter any more. Was *this* what she had been so afraid of? But no, it had been so much more. It had been everything, all of it, the intimacy and the need. 'I can't,' she said flatly. Ben stared at her, completely nonplussed. 'I'm dyslexic,' Natalia elaborated, her voice still flat and strangely loud in the yawning emptiness of the stadium. 'Severely so. I can barely read or write.'

Now Ben looked completely gobsmacked, his jaw slack, his eyes wide. It would have been amusing in any other circumstance. 'Why didn't you tell me?' he finally asked. 'I would have made concessions—'

'I didn't want concessions,' she told him. 'I never have. And in any case, only a few people know.' Her lips twisted in a humourless smile. 'It's a bit of a family secret.'

He shook his head, still flummoxed, not understanding. 'Why?'

She shrugged, not wanting to go into it or invite pity. 'Bad publicity,' she finally said, and he frowned, his eyebrows rising in disbelief.

'Your parents decided that? To keep it secret? Because of *publicity*? Didn't you—didn't you get any proper tutoring? There are a lot of ways to help dyslexia these days....'

Another shrug; her throat felt tight. Not getting the proper help had been the least of it. She wasn't going to tell him how her governess had locked her in a dark cupboard for being so slow to learn her letters, or how her teacher had mocked her repeatedly in front of her entire year. She wasn't going to explain how her parents had wanted it kept secret, since princesses didn't need much learning anyway, or how she always felt so slow and stupid and at least dressing up and going out had made her feel accomplished, even though she knew inside it was nothing. She couldn't say that even now she didn't want him to look at her differently, that she knew he'd thought she was strong and now she felt so weak.

She didn't say any of it, but then she didn't need to. She saw from Ben's thoughtful, narrowed gaze that he guessed it all, that he'd put the fragmented pieces of her life together in a way even she had never been able to.

'Thank you for telling me,' he finally said quietly. 'Thank you for being honest. That must have been hard.'

'It doesn't really matter now.'

'Oh?' His voice cooled, very slightly, but she could still tell. 'Why not?'

'I mean…' She gestured uselessly to the space between them. 'It doesn't matter to us. I was afraid to tell you… things…before, because I didn't want you to look at me differently. And I'm not used to telling anyone much of anything.'

'I've gathered that.'

'But it doesn't matter, because there can't be anything between us now, even if I—we—wanted there to be. I'm getting married.' The words felt weighted, like lead, falling so heavily into the stillness. 'It will be announced this week.'

'Ah, yes. Your marriage.' Ben nodded, and Natalia felt a sharp twist of unease. His voice sounded so very neutral. He nodded towards the newspaper. 'That's what I wanted you to look at actually, although there isn't really anything to read.' He gazed at her, his expression hard again, demanding something from her. 'You're not in the papers, Princess. Your sisters and brothers are, all over the place. But there's no mention of you or this groom of yours.'

'I told you, it hasn't been announced yet.'

'It hadn't even been decided yet,' Ben returned. 'Has it? Officially?'

She swallowed, her throat still tight and aching. 'It's being arranged—'

'*Being*. Yes. Because this is all quite recent, isn't it, Natalia? Six weeks ago you were engaged to the Prince of Montenavarre.'

'He called it off—'

'Funny, how royals can just do that.'

She stared at him. 'What are you trying to say, Ben?'

'What's your intended's name?'

'His name?'

'Yes. His name. His first name.'

For the life of her she couldn't think of it. 'He's the Sheikh of Qadirah—'

'His *name*, Princess.'

She felt impotent fury rise up in her. What was he trying to do? Prove? 'Khaled,' she finally said, a revealing note of triumph in her voice. 'His name is Khaled.'

'And this Khaled,' Ben asked, prowling close to her with a decisive, long-legged stride, 'does he know you?'

She took an inadvertent step backwards, her hip bumping the table. 'Know me?'

'Have you met?'

She lifted her chin. *Fine*. She'd answer all his questions. She had nothing left to hide. 'No, we haven't met yet, but we will this week.'

'So this Khaled doesn't know you,' Ben clarified. He stepped closer so she could feel the heat of him, smell the musk of his sweat and the tang of his aftershave. His knee nudged her thigh as she bumped against the table again, her back pressed against its hard edge.

'I just told you, we haven't met.'

'He doesn't, for example,' Ben continued, his voice dropping to a raw whisper, 'know that you go blotchy when you blush. Or that you're afraid of the dark.' She felt his hand, warm and strong, slide slowly, purposefully, up her bare thigh. She gasped aloud as his fingers slipped under her shorts, beneath her underwear, to her damp feminine heat. 'He doesn't know,' he continued, his voice dropping so low she could barely hear him, 'that you cry when you come.'

Natalia closed her eyes, tried to fight the intense wave of pleasure that rushed through her at the feeling of Ben's fingers pressed so intimately against her, knowing so specifically how to touch her.

'He doesn't know you like I do, Natalia,' Ben said, his fingers stroking her so persuasively. 'He never will.'

From somewhere she found words; they came out in short, staccato bursts, each one an effort. 'Perhaps he won't.'

'He won't,' Ben said, 'because you don't want him to.'

Her eyes fluttered open as she stared at him, his gaze blazing into hers. Her body hovered on that dazzling precipice and it would only take one more second, one more stroke, for her to find the release she was craving. Instinctively, unable to keep herself from doing so, she writhed under his caress, her body arching and seeking more, but he wouldn't give it to her.

'Ben...'

'You don't want him to,' Ben whispered, his fingers stilling, 'because it's so much easier that way, isn't it? So much safer.'

'I *can't*—'

'You can. You could say no to this marriage. Look at your sister Sophia. Your brother Alessandro. Haven't they done the same? You could do it if you wanted to, Natalia. If you wanted me.'

The truth of his words hammered into her heart, striking their decisive death blows. The shell she'd tried to rebuild over that fragile organ cracked and shattered again; Ben would never let it be otherwise. She knew he was right. She knew it with every inch of her being, every corner of her wounded heart. She hadn't fought this marriage because it was easier. It might be breaking her heart, but it was still easier. Even so, even now, she shook her head. 'No—'

'Yes.'

He stroked her one last time, slowly, lingeringly, and with a gasping cry her hips lifted of their own accord as she sought the fulfillment that he refused to give her. 'You see,' he said softly, withdrawing his hand, 'nobody likes to be toyed with.'

And he left her there, aching inside and out, as he headed towards the gates of the stadium.

Natalia doubled over, gasping as if she'd just run a sprint, her body protesting at how it had been used. She saw Ben walk away and somehow she found the strength to call after him. 'Kettle?' she shouted, her voice ringing through the empty stadium. 'Pot?'

He slowed, then stilled. After an interminable second he turned around. 'What,' he demanded, 'are you saying?'

'You're accusing me of not being honest enough, open enough. Not being willing to commit.' Her voice came out in ugly, raw gasps, tearing her throat. 'What about you, Ben? You do a nice dive in the goal box but I'm not really seeing it here, with me.'

'I told you—'

'You told me you *care*. You don't want to, you don't like it, but you care. Am I supposed to be doing cartwheels over that, hotshot?'

His gaze narrowed; she felt his fury. 'Later—'

'You told me you were willing to see if this thing between us works,' she reminded him rawly. 'What is that supposed to mean, Ben? Am I supposed to bare my soul, tear my family apart and risk losing everything I know for *that*?' He said nothing, just gave his head a little shake, although whether in denial or confusion or something else entirely Natalia didn't know. 'You're still in control,' she told him. 'You're still calling the shots. And until you let go as much as I have, until you reveal yourself the way I've been revealed, until you fight for me like no one else has, it's *not* worth it. And it never will be.' She stood, straightening her rumpled shorts, and with her head held high, her whole body trembling, she walked past him and through the stadium gates.

Ben stood by the gates, listening to them clang shut as Natalia walked through. In the distance he heard the slam of a car door, the roar of a motor. She was gone, and yet still he remained rooted here, her words—her accusations—echoing through him. *Until you let go as much as I have, until you*

*reveal yourself the way I've been revealed, until you fight for
me like no one else has, it's not worth it. And it never will be.*

They were hard words, angry and accusing. And true.
He hadn't given everything. He'd been pushing her to give,
demanding it of her, and yet he'd kept something back. The
strength of his feelings, the fears in his heart. He hadn't been
completely vulnerable, totally honest. Not like Natalia had.

No, Ben thought grimly, what he'd been was a hypocrite.
And Natalia, even in her hurt and humiliation and anger,
had seen it. Called him on it. The realisation filled him with
a scalding rush of shame, even as he loved her for that. He
loved her, full stop. And it was high time—if not too desperately, dangerously late—for him to tell her.

Natalia stared at her pale, waxen reflection in the mirror. She
looked terrible. The lavender evening gown she'd chosen for
tonight's dinner matched the livid shadows under her haunted
eyes. If Sheikh Khaled were present tonight, he'd most likely
cry off at the sight of her.

Sheikh Khaled. She couldn't summon the energy to feel
anything about her imminent engagement. She felt drained
and numb, although that blankness of emotion covered, she
feared, a deep and terrible sorrow. Her body still ached from
where Ben had touched her, and her mind reverberated with
the truth he'd spoken.

*He won't because you don't want him to. Because it's so
much easier that way, isn't it? So much safer. You could say
no to this marriage. You could do it if you wanted to, Natalia.
If you wanted me.*

With a shuddering sigh Natalia reached for some blush.
Ben had been right, but she had been as well. He'd demanded
everything from her, but he hadn't given it. He hadn't told
her he loved her. He hadn't laid bare his soul.

Yet should she have trusted that he *would*? Should she have

been brave enough to reject this planned marriage and cast
her lot—whatever it turned out to be—with Ben?

Her mind spun around and around, and came up with no
answers. She didn't know. She didn't know anything any
more. A knock sounded on the door and her maid, Ana,
peeked in.

'Your Highness? The queen wishes you to know that the
guests are arriving.'

'Thank you, Ana.' Slowly, her muscles aching, Natalia
stood. The dinner tonight was yet another state occasion, a
formal dinner with several nameless dignitaries. The queen
wanted Natalia visible at these kinds of functions before her
intended arrived, doing her royal duty. At last.

The king and queen were receiving guests in one of the
royal reception rooms, an elegant salon with frescoed walls
and marble pillars. Natalia stood stiffly among the guests, a
flute of untouched champagne clenched between her fingers,
trying to appear attentive as she listened to two ambassadors
discuss the rather depressing state of the economy in Europe.
She barely took in a word. Her heart felt like lead within her,
making her shoulders slump, her whole body sink. How could
she even keep herself upright with such a heavy heart?

Belatedly she realised the two ambassadors had paused
in their conversation, and the silence had gone on a little too
long. She struggled to think of something to say, only to see
that the two men weren't even paying attention to her. They
were looking towards the double doors at the front of the
salon, where a figure in an elegant tuxedo stood, his presence
innately commanding the attention of everyone in the room.
He stood with an assured sense of purpose that drew the focus
of the room, and felt like a jolt of electricity to Natalia's body.

It was Ben.

What was he doing here? He surely hadn't been invited.
Her parents had intended on a small gathering, a dozen
dignitaries, no more. Faces froze and shoulders drew up

haughtily as Ben came into the room. Clearly she wasn't the only one who knew he wasn't on the guest list.

What was he doing here?

His gaze surveyed the room and then arrowed in on her. Natalia felt her heart freeze in her chest, her fingers nerveless around her flute of champagne. She couldn't move, couldn't think, couldn't breathe. He started walking towards her, stopping about a metre away.

'What—' she said faintly, and stopped, heart and mind spinning.

'I've realised I have a few things to say to you,' Ben said, his voice low and melodious, flowing over her. 'Things I should have said, and want to say now.'

'What things?' Natalia whispered.

Ben glanced around at the small crowd of foreign officials, half whom were studiously ignoring them, the other half watching in riveted interest. 'Do you want me to say them here?' he asked. 'I will.'

Natalia didn't know whether that was a threat or a promise. She didn't know what *things* Ben intended on saying. 'I…I don't know.'

'I could say them somewhere more private,' Ben suggested, a tiny thread of humour in his voice. 'If you'll come with me.'

'Where?'

He gestured to the doors. 'Out.'

Natalia stared at him, saw the sincerity and something else blazing in his eyes. Something deeper. Could she walk out of this, walk right out on her parents and the palazzo, and go with Ben she didn't even know where?

Her heart thumped in her chest and she felt as dizzy as if she'd drunk a dozen glasses of champagne.

'Natalia?' Ben asked softly, and she heard the vulnerability in his voice that she'd felt so long in herself.

'Yes,' she said, her voice a thread, a wisp of sound. 'Yes, I'll come with you.'

She set her champagne on a tray and walked out of the
room, felt the gaze of a dozen people, of her parents, hard
on her back. At the door her mother stopped her, one hand
clutching her wrist.

'Natalia,' she warned. 'Where on earth do you think you're
going?'

Ben stepped between her and her mother. 'She's with me,'
he said, his voice as polite as ever, but very, very firm. Her
mother drew back, startled, and Ben led her out of the room.

Natalia let out an uncertain, trembling laugh as they
stepped out of the palazzo and the night enveloped them, as
soft as a lover's caress. 'So where are we going?' she asked.

'I could tell you, but then it wouldn't be a surprise.'

'True.' She hesitated and Ben turned to her, his hand outstretched.

'Do you want a surprise?'

'I don't know,' she admitted. 'I'm not sure I can take any
surprises right now.'

'I want to take you up in my plane,' Ben said, and Natalia
did not reply. She was thinking of the last time they'd been
in that tiny plane, how Ben had pushed her away from him.
The rejection still hurt, still made her doubt. 'Please,' he said,
and silently she nodded.

They didn't speak as they drove through the darkness to
the airfield. Ben's plane waited for them in a corner of the
tarmac, looking as tiny and intimate as ever. Natalia swallowed nervously as she climbed into the plane, grabbing a
handful of her long, swishy evening gown as she picked her
way across the cockpit in her high heels. Ben steadied her
with one hand before climbing in himself.

'This all feels so very familiar,' she said as she stared out
the window. She heard a sharp edge to her voice, an edge she
could not suppress.

'Familiar,' Ben agreed, 'but different too. I hope.' He
started the plane and Natalia leaned her head back against

the seat as they took off into the sky, leaving the lights of Santina twinkling far below.

They didn't speak for a long moment and Natalia felt a tension—and a tenuous hope—uncoil and tautly stretch inside her. 'So,' she finally said, breaking that endless silence. 'These things.'

'Yes.' Ben cleared his throat, and with a jolt Natalia realised he was nervous. 'I never told you why I've been so afraid of commitment.'

'OK.'

'My father cheated on my mother. You knew that. I knew that, even when I was small, and it made me so angry. I loved my dad. He was funny and charming and just…fun, really. Always laughing. When I realised he was weak and full of flaws too, I felt like I could almost hate him.' Natalia said nothing and Ben sighed. 'That's all rather expected, I know. Nothing new there. But what I haven't told you—didn't want to tell you—is that I also resented my mother, for taking him back. Over and over again, even though she knew. She knew about all his flings and affairs, and she just pretended like she didn't. It infuriated me. Still does, at least in part, if I'm going to be completely truthful. I wanted her to be strong. And I never wanted to be like her.'

'So,' Natalia said slowly, 'you avoided commitment because you were afraid of being weak, like her?'

'Yes, although I see now it takes a certain kind of strength to do what she has done. But as for you and me…' He let out a long, slow breath. 'From the moment I met you I felt like I was losing control. Wanting you. Wanting to know you, and for you to know me. And yet I avoided telling you anything really important about myself because I didn't want to feel weak. I tried to keep you the way I'd thought you were because I didn't want to get close. I didn't want to want you.'

Natalia gave him the ghost of a smile. 'Do you know how many times you've said that?'

'But the you I didn't want isn't the real you, Natalia.'

'Don't think too highly of me,' Natalia said quietly. Even now she couldn't keep from warning him off, just a bit. 'I've done a lot of things. Made a lot of mistakes.'

'Haven't we all? I certainly have. But I've seen you over the past few weeks. I've seen how you reach out to the kids on the pitch, how you're willing to be on their level. You haven't stood on being a princess.'

'Sometimes I don't want to be a princess.'

'And when I think how you worked in the office, without telling anyone about your dyslexia—'

'Don't,' she said, her voice catching. 'Don't pity me.'

Ben shook his head in vigorous denial. 'I admire you, Natalia. I always thought you were strong, but I had no idea. I still don't. You're amazing.'

The heartfelt sincerity in his tone humbled her; she couldn't doubt it. 'You're pretty amazing yourself,' she finally managed, her voice a bit choked, and he slid her a sideways smile.

'I'm not done yet.'

'No?'

'No.' He took a deep breath. 'What I really want to say is I love you. I love the woman you've been and the woman you've become. I love your strength and humour and grace, and how you never let me get away with anything. I love you, Natalia.'

She was going to cry. And she was wearing mascara. Laughing a little, Natalia dashed at her wet cheeks. 'I love you too,' she said quietly, and with comical exaggeration Ben cupped his ear.

'Sorry, what was that?'

She laughed and said it loudly. Shouted it. 'I love you!'

They were both silent, accepting and even reveling in the moment. Everything had been exposed; everything had been brought to the light. And it was good.

'I'm sorry for what I put you through,' Ben finally said quietly. 'I was so blind, in so many ways.'

'And I was afraid.'

'And now?'

She let out a shaky laugh. 'I'm not afraid. But I have no idea what's going to happen when I return to the palazzo. What my parents will say. Do.'

'You won't be alone,' Ben told her. 'I'll be by your side every second.'

She released a shuddering breath. 'I'm certainly glad for that.'

Natalia saw lights twinkling below them, and as Ben started to descend she wondered what their destination was. What would happen now.

She was not prepared for the sudden glare of lights as Ben maneuvered the Seabird towards the ground. She peered out the window and saw a bridge lit by lamplight and near-swarming with people.

'Where are we?' she asked. 'Why are they so many people?'

'The Ponte Milvio Bridge in Rome.'

'You're landing a plane on the *bridge*?' The Ponte Milvio was over two thousand years old, in the centre of Rome, and local legend told that any couple who got engaged on the bridge would be assured lifelong health and happiness.

'The Seabird lands like a helicopter,' Ben explained. 'And I cleared it with the local authorities beforehand.'

Natalia peered out of the window. She could see the Tiber River awash with lights from the city, the ancient bridge looming nearer and crowded with people.

'Who are all those people?' she asked.

'Ah. Well.' Ben shot her a rather rueful grin. 'They're reporters.'

'Paparazzi?'

'There are a few legitimate journalists in there as well.'

Natalia shook her head, not understanding. 'Why would

they all be on the bridge? How on earth could they know we'd be here?' She hadn't even known herself.

'They might,' Ben said, 'have received a tip-off.'

Natalia stared at him blankly. She didn't understand why Ben was so insouciant about such a huge thing when a few short weeks ago the possibility of just one reporter had had him pushing her away from him as quickly as he could. Comprehension came like a thunderclap. 'You rang them? *You* tipped them off?'

'I might have done.'

'Why?'

'I want the whole world to know how I feel about you, Natalia. That I love you.'

She let out a choked laugh, hardly able to believe this was real. 'And if I didn't want any reporters?' she couldn't help but ask, and he looked a little abashed.

'I'm afraid, in this one instance, you have no choice. But in future I'll guard our privacy with extreme care, I promise.'

In future. The words caused a bubble of happiness to rise inside of her, shiny and translucent. 'So just what are you going to tell these reporters?'

'First things first.' He reached for her and, surprised, Natalia came to him. His arms enfolded her and his lips found hers. Outside, the reporters were shouting in agitation and excitement, desperate to get a decent snap. Natalia pulled away.

'We are going to be on the front page of every paper from here to New York.'

'I don't mind.'

She stared at him. 'Really?'

'Really.' He gave her a wry smile. 'In this one instance anyway. I want to show you I mean what I say. I love you and I'm happy for the whole world to know it.'

'I love you too,' Natalia said softly.

'And then there's this.' Ben fished in his pocket and produced a small box of black velvet. 'Natalia Santina, princess of my heart, will you make me the happiest man in the world and marry me?'

Natalia blinked back tears as she gazed at the antique diamond surrounded by a circle of luminescent pearls. 'Yes. Yes, I will.'

He slid the gorgeous ring on her finger and then nodded towards the still-shouting paparazzi outside. 'Then perhaps we should go and make an announcement before I whisk you away again. I can't wait to tell the world about my wife-to-be.'

Smiling, tears of joy still sparkling in her eyes, Natalia took his hand as she followed him out of the plane.

EPILOGUE

NATALIA was amazed at how easy everything became, with Ben at her side. Her parents were surprisingly and touchingly accepting of her engagement to Ben; her father King Eduardo said he could see how much Ben loved her. Even the Sheikh of Qadriah took the refusal of his offer with grace, laughingly saying he could hardly compete with a man who proposed with such style—and so publicly.

They were married six weeks later, on a secluded beach on Santina, with no photographers or reporters in attendance. A single photograph of her and Ben was sold to a respectable newspaper for a six-figure sum that was donated to a charity for helping those with learning disabilities. After years of shameful silence, Natalia went public with her own dyslexia and was now on the board of the charity and receiving tutoring herself to help her with reading and writing skills.

Their future felt as bright and newly minted as the sun that rose in the pearly pink dawn sky the morning after their wedding. Natalia stood in front of the sliding glass door in Ben's beach house, watching the sun rise higher and higher in the sky, growing in heat and radiance, spreading its healing rays across the earth.

Ben came up behind her, slipping his arms around her waist, and kissed her neck before resting his chin on her head.

'I'm just thinking about that bet of ours,' she said, and she heard him chuckle.

'And?'

'I won.'

'So you did.'

'You're mine to command for the day,' she reminded him.

'For the day,' Ben agreed, 'and for ever.'

Natalia smiled, happiness buoying her soul. 'Then let's begin,' she said, and turned to kiss him.

* * * * *

*Enjoy an exclusive excerpt from the next book
in* THE SANTINA CROWN *miniseries!*

THE MAN BEHIND THE SCARS *by Caitlin Crews*

* * *

LOOKING around, Angel also automatically excluded any men with women already hanging off them, or even standing too close to them, as she didn't have the time or inclination to compete, and anyway, she wasn't at all interested in someone *else's* husband.

She might have descended to following in her mother's footsteps and becoming a shameless gold digger, she thought piously, but she did have *some* standards.

She took care to avoid any of the Jackson family, Chantelle and Izzy included—or perhaps especially—as she moved through the crowd. Those she was particularly close to—like the bride-to-be Allegra herself or Ben, the eldest Jackson sibling and as close to a big brother as Angel was likely to get—she was determined to avoid at all costs.

She couldn't handle any sort of show of concern, not from the people she actually considered near enough to family. She didn't want any of them to ask her how she was doing, because she might accidentally let the awful truth slip out in all its ugliness, and that would hardly put her in the right frame of mind to catch a husband, would it?

Not that she had any idea what frame of mind that was meant to be, she thought wryly, slipping behind another pillar to avoid a tight scrum of what, to her untrained eye, looked like a pack of highly disapproving priests. Or possibly bankers.

HPEX0812CONT

And that was when she saw him.

He was lurking—there was no better word for it—almost in the shadows of the next pillar, all by himself, presenting Angel with a view of his commanding profile. He was…magnificent. That was also the best word for it. For him. She paused for a moment, letting her eyes travel all over him.

His shoulders were wide and strong, and his torso looked like packed steel beneath a suit that should have been elegant, but on his lean, rugged frame was instead…something else. Something that whispered of great power, ruthlessly and not altogether seamlessly contained. He stood with his feet apart and his hands thrust into the pockets of his trousers, and she got the impression that there was something almost belligerent in that stance, something profoundly dangerous.

Every hair on her body seemed to stand on end.

There was just something about him, Angel thought unsteadily as another kind of thunder seemed to roll through her then, making her breath seem harder to catch than it should have been.

She couldn't manage to look away. Maybe it was his thick dark hair, too long to be strictly correct and at distinct and intriguing odds with the conservative suit he wore. Maybe it was the brooding, considering way he looked out over the ballroom, as if he saw nothing at all to catch his interest, nothing to combat whatever it was he carried inside him, like a deep shadow within yet almost visible to the naked eye. Maybe it was that lean jaw, and the grim mouth that Angel suddenly felt was some kind of challenge, though she couldn't have said why.

Whatever else this man was, she thought then, anticipation and adrenaline coursing through her, making her whole body seem to hum into alertness, he was a candidate. She moved toward him, pleased to note that the closer she got, the more impressive he was. There was a certain watchful stillness to him that she felt like an echo beneath her ribs. She wasn't at all surprised when he turned his head to pin her with a cold, dark stare while she was still several feet away—and she got the sudden and distinct impression that he'd sensed her approach from the start, from the moment she'd laid eyes on him. As if he was preternaturally *aware* of everything that happened around him.

For a moment, she saw nothing but that stare.

Cold gray eyes, the most remote she'd ever seen, and darker than anyone's ought to be. He seemed to see into her, through her, as if she was entirely transparent. As if she was made of some insubstantial bit of glass. As if he could read her desperation, her dreams, her plans and her flimsy hopes, in a single, searing glance. She *felt* it, him, everywhere.

She blinked—and then she saw his scars.

A wide, devastating set of once angry, now simply brutal scars swiped across the whole left side of his face, raking him from temple to chin, sparing his eye but ravaging the rest of the side of his face and carrying on to loop under his hard, masculine chin. She sucked in a shocked breath, but she didn't stop walking. She couldn't, somehow, as if he compelled her. As if he had already pulled her in and she was only bowing to the inevitable.

* * *

Available in August 2012 from Harlequin Presents®.

COMING NEXT MONTH from Harlequin Presents®
AVAILABLE JULY 31, 2012

#3077 THE SECRETS SHE CARRIED
Lynne Graham
Erin and Christophe's passionate affair ended harshly.
Years later, he's bent on revenge, until Erin drops two very
important bombshells!

#3078 THE MAN BEHIND THE SCARS
The Santina Crown
Caitlin Crews
Rafe McFarland—Earl of Pembroke and twenty-first-century
pinup—has secretly wed tabloid darling Angel in the newest
Santina scandal!

#3079 HIS REPUTATION PRECEDES HIM
The Lyonedes Legacy
Carole Mortimer
Eva is hired to decorate Markos Lyonedes's apartment, but
the notorious playboy makes it difficult for her to stay out of
the bedroom!

#3080 DESERVING OF HIS DIAMONDS?
The Outrageous Sisters
Melanie Milburne
Billionaire Emilio Andreoni needs one thing: the perfect
woman. That was once Gisele Carter until headline-grabbing
scandals made her the not-so-perfect fiancée!

#3081 THE MAN SHE SHOULDN'T CRAVE
Lucy Ellis
Dating agency owner Rose is in over her head with a new PR
proposal involving ruthless Russian ice-hockey team owner
Plato Kuragin!

#3082 PLAYING THE GREEK'S GAME
Sharon Kendrick
Few dare to defy global hotel magnate Zac Constantinides—
but he's met his match in feisty designer Emma!

You can find more information on upcoming Harlequin®
titles, free excerpts and more at www.Harlequin.com.

HPCNM0712

REQUEST YOUR
FREE BOOKS!

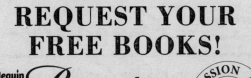

Harlequin *Presents*

PASSION GUARANTEED SEDUCTION

2 FREE NOVELS PLUS
2 FREE GIFTS!

YES! Please send me 2 FREE Harlequin Presents® novels and my 2 FREE gifts (gifts are worth about $10). After receiving them, if I don't wish to receive any more books, I can return the shipping statement marked "cancel." If I don't cancel, I will receive 6 brand-new novels every month and be billed just $4.30 per book in the U.S. or $4.99 per book in Canada. That's a saving of at least 14% off the cover price! It's quite a bargain! Shipping and handling is just 50¢ per book in the U.S. and 75¢ per book in Canada.* I understand that accepting the 2 free books and gifts places me under no obligation to buy anything. I can always return a shipment and cancel at any time. Even if I never buy another book, the two free books and gifts are mine to keep forever.

106/306 HDN FERQ

Name _____ (PLEASE PRINT) _____

Address _____ Apt. #

City _____ State/Prov. _____ Zip/Postal Code

Signature (if under 18, a parent or guardian must sign)

Mail to the **Reader Service:**
IN U.S.A.: P.O. Box 1867, Buffalo, NY 14240-1867
IN CANADA: P.O. Box 609, Fort Erie, Ontario L2A 5X3

Not valid for current subscribers to Harlequin Presents books.

**Are you a current subscriber to Harlequin Presents books
and want to receive the larger-print edition?
Call 1-800-873-8635 or visit www.ReaderService.com.**

* Terms and prices subject to change without notice. Prices do not include applicable taxes. Sales tax applicable in N.Y. Canadian residents will be charged applicable taxes. Offer not valid in Quebec. This offer is limited to one order per household. All orders subject to credit approval. Credit or debit balances in a customer's account(s) may be offset by any other outstanding balance owed by or to the customer. Please allow 4 to 6 weeks for delivery. Offer available while quantities last.

Your Privacy—The Reader Service is committed to protecting your privacy. Our Privacy Policy is available online at www.ReaderService.com or upon request from the Reader Service.

We make a portion of our mailing list available to reputable third parties that offer products we believe may interest you. If you prefer that we not exchange your name with third parties, or if you wish to clarify or modify your communication preferences, please visit us at www.ReaderService.com/consumerschoice or write to us at Reader Service Preference Service, P.O. Box 9062, Buffalo, NY 14269. Include your complete name and address.

HP11B